THE FACE OF VENGEANCE

He pulled her to him, drawing her close. Her eyes were closed, her entire attention given to the romance of the moment. They did not speak again, and there was only the rustle of the leafy canopy overhead, and the sweet sounds of summer.

There was a slight noise, a mere diversion from the whisper of the breeze in the trees. Lazily, Madeline LaFontaine opened her eyes. To her utter horror, there was a face looking down into hers . . . the face of a tall, muscular native. He was nearly naked, and his expression radiated hatred.

He was in the act of lifting a spear high overhead with both hands.

"Baptiste!" she screamed, but he did not even have time to turn and look before the lance descended. . . .

Bantam Books by Don Coldsmith
Ask your bookseller for the books you have missed

Fort de Chastaigne

»»»»»»»»»»»»»»»»»»»»»

D O N C O L D S M I T H

BANTAM BOOKS
NEW YORK · TORONTO · LONDON · SYDNEY · AUCKLAND

All of the characters in this book are fictitious,
and any resemblance to actual persons, living or
dead, is purely coincidental.

*This edition contains the complete text
of the original hardcover edition.
NOT ONE WORD HAS BEEN OMITTED.*

FORT DE CHASTAIGNE

*A Bantam Domain Book / published by arrangement with
Doubleday*

*PRINTING HISTORY
Doubleday edition published April 1990
Bantam edition / December 1991*

ISBN 0-553-29419-9

Published simultaneously in the United States and Canada

PRINTED IN THE UNITED STATES OF AMERICA

RAD   0 9 8 7 6 5 4 3 2 1

Time period: Early 1700s, a few years after *Song of the Rock*

Introduction

>> >> >>

During the early 1700s, France established several forts around the junction of the Kansas and Missouri Rivers, now the area of Kansas City. There were several exploratory probes such as the one described here, and France did carry on a limited trade with Spain in Santa Fe for some years.

"Fort de Chastaigne" is a fictional place, but the description leans heavily on that of Fort de Cavagnial, which was located northwest of present Fort Leavenworth. All of these sites were abandoned within a few decades, because of lengthy supply lines, as well as many of the problems encountered in this fictional account. The area later became part of the Louisiana Purchase of 1803.

DON COLDSMITH
1989

Fort
de
Chastaigne

»»»» »»»» »»»» » » »

1
» » »

In all his thirty-odd summers, White Fox could remember no Sun Dance that seemed so exciting. The very air seemed alive, and the People thrilled with the annual celebration. They laughed and talked and renewed acquaintances, raced horses and gambled with the plum stones or played the stick game. The storytellers, around the story-fires, held the attention of young and old alike until far into the night. Through several nights prior to the Sun Dance itself, fires burned until dawn. The People seemed reluctant to go to bed, lest something exciting might happen and they would miss it.

White Fox was not certain why the excitement was running so high this season. It was an unusual location, to be sure, much farther east and somewhat farther north than usual. For years, the Eastern band had complained about the location of the Sun Dance. They always had to travel longer distances than anyone else, they protested.

It was not true, of course. Both the Mountain and Red Rocks bands usually had a longer journey.

However, at the Big Council last season, someone tired of listening to the arguments had suggested this site. At least it would stop the complaints of the Eastern band for a few seasons. Possibly, someone else noted, the Eastern band could even arrive on time, if the Sun Dance was held in their own territory. There was general laughter. Even the Eastern band, accustomed to being the butt of the jokes each season, entered in. Sometimes it seemed to White Fox that there were many in the Eastern band who actually enjoyed their reputation for foolishness, which went back for generations. There had been leaders of great ability from this band, of course. Red Feather, White Fox's ancestor, had been a wise chief. Still, Fox had always been glad that his immediate family was identified with the Southern band, rather than the Eastern.

As it happened, the Eastern band was still actually the next-to-last to arrive at the site. Only the far-off Red Rocks arrived later, and that was quite excusable. Their territory was far to the southwest. The arrival of the Red Rocks initiated one of the most spectacular demonstrations seen for a generation. The newcomers heralded their arrival with a mock attack on the camp. From the crest of the ridge to the south, the young horsemen swept down on the scattered lodges of the summer camp, yelling the throaty war cry of the People at the top of their lungs.

"What is it?" cried South Wind in alarm, as she popped out of the lodge, face distorted with concern.

"It is nothing," laughed her husband. "The Red Rocks have arrived."

"It is good," the woman answered nervously, seemingly not quite convinced.

White Fox watched her move back inside. How difficult for her, even after all these years. Sixteen, now? He had tried to imagine the many strange things that Wind had been forced to learn since their marriage. She had been raised by her deaf-mute grandfather, a half-crazy old recluse, and had never heard spoken words until White Fox had found her, living alone in the cave. It must be terrifying for her, even now, to hear unexpectedly the resounding war cries of the People from the exuberant young men. The horsemen were circling the camp now, still yelling. Some of the young warriors from other bands were swinging up on their own horses now to join the wild abandon of the riders.

Red Horse came trotting up, his eyes glistening with excitement.

"Father, may I ride with them?"

White Fox started to refuse, but paused. Why not? The boy was as old as he himself had been on the trading expedition to Santa Fe . . . *aiee*, that seemed long ago!

"Go ahead, my son," he agreed.

Red Horse sprinted away, and South Wind looked out of the lodge again.

"Is this wise, my husband?" she asked in concern.

"Yes, Wind, he is nearly grown now. Let him join the others. They will ride a few times around, and then stop."

"I suppose so," she agreed.

Already, irate women at the upwind side of the village were yelling at the horsemen to move out farther. The dust and dirt raised by a hundred or more pounding hooves was drifting across the camp, threatening racks of drying meat and other foods in process of preparation.

"Go along, stupid ones," an old woman shouted, waving them away. "Have you no mothers, to teach you manners?"

White Fox and South Wind watched their son leap to his horse and join the yelling circle.

"He rides well," Fox observed.

"Yes. He reminds me of you when I first saw you," she smiled. *"Aiee,* how can he be grown already?"

White Fox took her hand, and they watched the mad race for a moment.

"I was thinking a moment ago," he admitted. "He is about the age I was when we were caught in the war in Santa Fe."

"But I did not know you then," she smiled. "Were you so grown-up as he?"

"I thought I was," he mused, "as he thinks he is, I suppose."

A group of three or four riders swept past, yelling a slightly different war cry, a yipping falsetto.

"Who are they?" Wind asked.

"Head Splitters, maybe. They come with the Red Rocks sometimes."

These allies, once enemies of the People, had no Sun Dance of their own. However, they seemed to appreciate the atmosphere and excitement, and often attended or even participated in the ceremonies of the People. At times, in the western portion of the People's range, whole bands of Head Splitters would join the camp for this festival of life-renewal.

"Do you think there are more visitors this year?" asked South Wind.

"Not Head Splitters," Fox said. "Others, maybe. We are in new territory for the Sun Dance, on the River of Swans here. There will be curious tribes, and we are at peace with nearly everyone. There are Growers downstream, and Pawnees along the Big River. Mandans beyond that. Any of them might decide to come and watch."

He noticed a slightly anxious look cross her face.

"It is all right, Wind," he assured her.

She smiled.

"Yes, yes. But, you know, half my life, Grandfather taught me to fear everyone."

He nodded. She had done quite well to overcome that start.

"You do enjoy their stories," he teased.

She laughed.

"Yes, I do. That part is wonderful. I grew up with Grandfather's stories, and never knew there were others."

"And they were in hand-signs," he reminded.

Both laughed, and she leaned against him.

"My husband," she said thoughtfully, "I have thought many times how good that you were the one who found me."

"Yes, it is good."

The circle of yelling attackers was now beginning to break up. The main column of the Red Rocks band was straggling over the ridge, and young horsemen would have other duties to perform. Red Horse slid from his mare, removed the thong from her lower jaw, and released her to graze with the herd. Now he came back toward his parents' lodge, still flushed with excitement.

"Father," he began, "the real-chief asked me to tell you . . . he will call the Big Council tomorrow night, if the time is right for you."

"It is good," agreed White Fox. "Would you go and tell him?"

Red Horse nodded and trotted off. There were times when the young man was so great a help that it was all his father could do to avoid urging him to become his apprentice. White Fox would need an assistant some day, but it must be the decision of the young man, not a choice made for him. In addition, it was a calling, a gift of the spirit. The recipient could refuse, but must first be selected. Ah, well, time would tell whether young Red Horse might qualify to succeed his father as a holy man. The gift had come quite late to White Fox.

As a medicine man, Fox had no major function in the Big Council. However, the timing of the Sun Dance was important, and it must be linked closely. It was traditional to begin the three-day announcement by the holy men on the day after the Big Council, so close cooperation was customary.

The family of the real-chief was already supervising the construction of the Sun Dance lodge, an open-sided brush arbor that would shade the dancers by day. The Sun Dance bull had been secured, and the construction of the effigy that would wear its skin and head was under way.

By the time the shadows were lengthening, the newcomers had begun to settle in their assigned place in the camp circle, and to establish their lodges for the temporary stay. South Wind prepared the evening meal for her husband and son and the three of them ate. The two younger children had gone to the lodge of their grandparents for the day.

Red Horse finished hurriedly and rose. It would be an exciting evening, with many old friends and relatives, as well as interesting strangers among the visitors. It would be the last night before the intense and constant ceremonies began, and many would be relaxing tonight in the informality of the evening. They watched Red Horse join some of his friends and move in search of excitement.

"Will you walk with me?" asked South Wind seriously. "I will see you very little for several sleeps, after tonight."

"Of course. You mean in the camp, or alone?" South Wind giggled.

"I meant in the camp. But, let us go and watch the sunset together. Then we can come back to the story-fires."

2

>> >> >>

Quite possibly there were two main reasons for the extra excitement of this Sun Dance. One was the location, with its own contribution in the form of new visitors who had never seen the ceremony.

The other was simply that the weather had been magnificent. There were those among the People who held that the Moon of Roses was the most beautiful of the year anyway. It would be hard to discredit such a theory. The clean clear blue of the sky with the occasional towering mushroom of a thunderhead reflecting the white rays of Sun Boy's new torch . . . *aiee*, it was good. The greening of the prairie was complete, the flowers were blooming in profusion. Even Rain Maker, at this time, seemed benevolent in his work, using soft warm rains that seemed to bless the return of the grass and the buffalo. Later, in the Moon of Thunder, Rain Maker's drum and his spears of real-fire would be a different matter, but for now . . . well, it was good.

The entire sequence of the annual celebration must have seemed slow and disorganized to those who had never seen it. The casual gathering of the bands, the carefree acceptance of late arrivals. This was an extension of the way of the People. From generations during which they had little control, these children of the plains had developed a day-at-a-time, easygoing tolerance of the world. Seen overall, there was much more formality to the Sun Dance festival than one might assume. It began with the pleasure of social interaction and renewal of friendships, with the prairie's own renewal. From there, the festival accelerated through the several days of formal ceremony to the climactic last day, when the last of the prayers and major sacrifices were offered. The final supplications for good health and good hunting, expressions of thanksgiving and of patriotism, the fulfillment of vows made last season, would be finally accomplished. The People would scatter again for the season, after choosing next year's site for the ceremony.

White Fox watched the excitement in a detached way, though he felt it deeply. It was not fitting to the dignity of the holy man's office to become too involved in the foolishness of the occasion. In a short while his responsibilities in the Sun Dance itself would begin, but for now . . . He shifted comfortably against the back rest and blew a mouthful of fragrant smoke into the breeze. Life was pleasant, and his heart was good.

Red Horse approached, moving at the half-trot that had always seemed more suited to him than a walk. Even as a small child, the boy had seemed to lope at play, with this odd lopsided skip-step. It had soon been apparent that he was pretending to be a horse. This was partially responsible for his present name. This, and the fascination that the youngster had always had for the animals. Red Horse. How it seemed to fit the boy. Probably, Fox thought, unless some event of great importance occurred to cause a change, this one would remain Red Horse for life.

As he had approached maturity, Red Horse's walking gait had been used more often. It was still amusing to his parents, however, that in times of excitement he became a child again, half-trotting from one place to another in the sheer excitement of being alive.

Red Horse trotted up to where his father sat, and stopped, breathing only slightly faster from the exertion.

"Father," he said, "there are strangers coming."

White Fox looked at the young man, puzzled. Of course there were strangers, visitors from many tribes. It was expected.

"Yes?" asked White Fox, waiting. There must be more.

"Well, I . . . No, Father, these are different. They come from far away. Northeast, it is said."

"Yes," agreed the holy man. "River People?"

There were tribes who lived largely along the big rivers, depending heavily on fishing as well as growing and occasional hunting. The People seldom had contact with such tribes, as their own was the culture of the prairie and the buffalo. The River People would seem strange to young Red Horse, who had never had contact with them before. But the young man was shaking his head.

"No, no, Father, not the River People. These are outsiders."

"What do they look like?" asked White Fox.

This was a puzzling conversation, he thought.

"Well . . ." began Red Horse hesitantly. "I have not seen them," he finally admitted. "But our wolves say . . ."

"*Aiee!*" exclaimed his father. "You have not even *seen* these strangers?"

He did not feel quite the ridicule that he was expressing. This was apparently a special situation. The scouts of the People were interpreting the approach of the strangers as something quite important. These scouts, experienced hunters and warriors, were referred to as "wolves," after the big gray hunters who followed the traveling buffalo herds, constantly circling the periphery of the main body.

White Fox's mood softened.

"What do our wolves say?" he asked in a gentler tone.

"That these are outsiders from a far tribe, Father. Like our grandfathers, maybe? Or the Metal People?"

A strange feeling of apprehension crept up between Fox's shoulder blades and settled at the base of his skull. It was a chill that set his neckhairs erect. Memory swept back through the years, to the time when he was the age of young Red Horse. A trading party of the People had become entangled in the war between the Metal People and those of the pueblos. White Fox and his father, Red Feather, had spent many days in a cage in Santa Fe, and before it was over much blood had been shed. Sometimes even yet, Fox had nightmares about the trapped feeling in that lodge with the iron bars on the windows.

The People had returned to the old ways, believing that while such hostilities were likely, the rewards were not worth the risks. They had elected not to trade to the southwest for the metal tools and weapons that had once seemed so important. It was probably not even possible now that the Metal People had been driven south, entirely out of the area, by the followers of Popé, the holy man of the Tewas pueblos. There had been no contact since, and the People had sought none.

But this situation was different. These men, it seemed, had come from the northeast. As far as White Fox could remember, none of the Spanish . . . the Metal People . . . had ever been known in that direction. But there had been others. His own grandfather, he recalled, was of this other tribe. Woodchuck, the man had been called. He was an outsider, a warrior who had come to explore and had married among the People. Ah, yes, he remembered more now. There were two of them, these warriors. The other was called Sky-Eyes, from an odd color, like that of a blind man: *blue* eyes rather than normal color. White Fox remembered these men from his childhood. Yes, Sky-Eyes had been the husband of the great medicine-woman Pale Star.

These men had come from the northeast, a tribe different from that of the Spanish. Could it be that the strangers of whom the wolves spoke were of the same tribe? Ah, there had been another expedition, Fox now recalled, when he was quite small. A chief called Worm-Face, from a hairy growth on his lip which resembled a caterpillar. That one had been honored and respected by the People. White Fox could remember little more.

He wished he could talk to Looks Far, his teacher and advisor. But Looks Far, advanced in years, had crossed over shortly after White Fox had finished his apprenticeship to the holy man. It had been as if Looks Far, now able to relinquish his responsibilities, had simply decided on the time of his death.

Pale Star might have been even better to talk to, for this purpose. She had been a master of language, able to speak the tongue of her husband

and Woodchuck as well as a dozen others, it was said. But she was gone too. The grand old lady, still beautiful in the dignity of her old age, had crossed over only three winters back. It was said that she had seen more than eighty winters.

Then who, White Fox wondered. Who would know? The answer came to him quickly, and he wondered why he had not thought of it sooner. Of course! His own father, Red Feather, had traded with the Spanish and knew their ways, but had also dealt with the other, the . . . *Fran-cois!* Yes, that was it . . . French!

White Fox rose.

"Come, my son," he said. "Let us find your grandfather."

3
>> >> >>

Red Feather sat comfortably, smoking before his lodge.

"*Ah-koh*, Uncle," his son greeted, using the customary term of respect due an older male of the People.

Red Feather motioned White Fox and Red Horse to be seated.

"Father," White Fox now began more informally, "Horse tells me there are visitors coming from the northeast."

Red Feather nodded.

"There are many visitors this year," he agreed. "It is good."

He settled back to smoke, apparently unconcerned.

"No, no, these are outsiders from far away," explained White Fox. "Maybe French."

Red Feather quickly sat upright.

"They come in boats, Grandfather," offered Red Horse.

"Boats? You did not tell me that!" White Fox exclaimed.

"No matter," the older man grunted, "but tell me now, Horse. You saw these men?"

"No, Grandfather, I only heard of it. The wolves told it."

Red Feather and White Fox exchanged glances. So far it had seemed that the story of outsiders traveling toward the meeting place of the Sun Dance was only that . . . a story. Rumors were always rampant at any tribal gathering. It was, perhaps, a natural outgrowth of the coming together of large numbers of the People. There was competition, though it might be unconscious, to tell the best stories, the most exciting news. This led to a tendency to exaggerate, and the stories became larger and more exciting. The next storyteller, hoping to surpass that of the last, would in turn stretch his tale to the limits of credibility. Soon one did not know what to believe.

In this case, however, both of the older men were quick to pay attention to rumors of outsiders. Both had reason to do so. Both men, at the time of the pueblo war, had spent time in a Spanish jail. It had been largely a misunderstanding, but such misunderstandings happen when different cultures meet. They had been there in Santa Fe only to trade, as they had done for a generation. But the natives of the area had distrusted them because of this trade with the Spanish.

Meanwhile, they were also burdened with Spanish distrust. By the time the land exploded into bloody violence, the Spanish no longer trusted *any* native of any tribe. The People had been fortunate to escape with small loss of life.

But, back beyond this, the memory of Red Feather reached even farther. The old warrior was nearing fifty winters now, but sometimes it seemed only yesterday that he was shot, nearly fatally, in an earlier misunderstanding. Only the skill of the pueblo holy men had enabled him to survive at all. It had been ironic that his wound was inflicted, though in Spanish territory, by one of a French exploring party. Even more strange, these travelers had been of the far-off country of his own father, Woodchuck, who had married here and become one of the People. As he recalled, some of that exploring party had actually been known to Woodchuck. There was much that Red Feather did not remember, because he had lain near death for a long time. Also, when he did begin to recover, he had fallen in love. With his head filled with thoughts of Moon Flower, there was no room to think of such less important things as French, Spanish, and gunshot wounds from the smoke poles.

Red Feather smiled to himself. *Aiee,* were the People destined to encounter such contacts again and again, with each generation? It was not all bad, of course. These contacts were productive of newer and better things, better and easier lives. Had the People not acquired the first horse in this way? Long, long ago, the legendary Heads Off had appeared from the south, riding the First Elk-dog. This had forever changed the ways of the People. It was almost forgotten now, that the People once hunted and traveled on foot, and were poor, and often starved to death in the winter Moon of Hunger, before the coming of the horse. There were still those, including his own family, who proudly traced their ancestry to Heads Off.

Other contacts with the outsiders had resulted in acquisition of metal tools and weapons. There were knives and spear points and arrowheads, as well as the fire-starter which produced sparks when struck by a flint. Of course, at each new step, there had been those who objected. Any present troubles that the People might have at such a time were sure to be blamed on whatever was new. The old women clucked their tongues over a season of drought or poor hunting, and insisted that it was because of the new ways. If the People had continued to make fire by the rubbing sticks, the old ones said, instead of with the flint and metal, then the season's bad luck would not have occurred. Many did continue to use the traditional sticks, but most thought it made no difference. Fire is fire.

Similarly, long ago, Red Feather had heard, there was a question about meat. Meat sliced to dry with a metal knife would spoil more easily, it was thought, than if prepared with a traditional flint blade. Gradually that idea had died. It was now accepted by all but the most reactionary that some meat spoils sometimes, regardless.

Red Feather wondered if there had always been such a question with each new custom. Probably. He could visualize that there may have even been some who resisted the use of the elk-dog in hunting buffalo. Probably hunger had cured that objection.

"Grandfather?" Horse was saying.

"What? Oh, yes . . . What did you say, Horse?"

"I asked if there is something we should do. Should I go and find out about these men?"

The two older men exchanged glances again. There was some apprehension in both. Such an innocent thing could become dangerous very quickly.

"I think not, Horse," advised his grandfather. "Let the wolves watch them. If they are coming here, we will soon see them. Go, now, ride with your friends. I would speak with your father."

Red Horse turned away, but White Fox called to him.

"Horse!"

"Yes, Father?"

"My son, listen to your grandfather, and to me.

You are not to go to see these travelers. Not until they come here, to the camp. Understood?"

"Yes, Father."

It was apparent that the young man was disappointed, but they knew he would not disobey. It was not his way. Any troubles that Red Horse had ever had in his growing up were those of mischief or of curiosity. There had been no disobedience. There seldom was, among the People, but even less than average in this boy. He turned and moved away.

"It is good," observed Red Feather. "Tell me, Fox, do you expect him to follow you as a holy man?"

"*Aiee*, I do not know, Father. His head is full of questions, but he has given no hint."

Red Feather nodded.

"Nor did you, my son. I was surprised when you chose to follow Looks Far. There had been no medicine man in our family for a long while."

The holy man chuckled.

"Yes, I know. I was surprised too, Father. But my vision-quest, the Rock . . ."

"Yes, that was a powerful quest," agreed Red Feather. "It found you a wife, too . . . but enough. Tell me, Fox, what you think of this tale of men in boats."

"I . . . I do not know, Father. That is why I came. These strangers, if it is really true, of course, are probably not Spanish. What then? French?"

"Maybe so. We have seen no French for a generation, though."

"I have never seen them," Fox pointed out. "There are few who have. But *you* have, Father. *Aiee . . .*" He paused to think for a moment. ". . . Is it that your father was one of them?"

Red Feather nodded.

"Yes. Woodchuck, and Sky-Eyes also. They came as warriors of the French and decided to stay."

"Ah, that is as I remembered. Do you speak their tongue, Father?"

"No. No one does, now, I think. I have only Spanish, and it is many snows since we used that. But, they may use hand-signs. If, of course, there are men in boats at all. Someone may have seen a Mandan fishing, or even a Pawnee. They sometimes use the bull-boats, do they not?"

"Maybe so. But Father . . . I cannot explain it, but I am made to think that this is no rumor, no mistake. This is important."

Red Feather nodded thoughtfully.

"This does not surprise me. Yours is the gift of medicine. Have you made your ceremonies, used your bones?"

"No, Father, I only just learned of this, and wanted to speak with you about it."

He rose and turned to face his father again.

"I will go and cast the bones," he stated. "If I learn more, I will return."

Red Feather watched him go. *Yes*, he thought, *I*

can feel it too, my son. There is something important here.

He hoped it would not prove harmful or dangerous to the People. He was getting too old for such things.

4
>> >> >>

None among the People had ever seen boats like these before. The only boats in their experience were the small round bull-boats used by the Mandans and other tribes along the rivers. Such a boat was made of a single buffalo hide, stretched and shaped while soft, on a wooden hoop. It was perfectly round, flat-bottomed, and its size was limited to the largest bull hide available. One or two people, with a minimum of baggage, was its load. Still, it was useful sometimes in crossing the prairie rivers.

The boats of the strangers brought exclamations of awe. They were long and narrow, high in front and back, and carried eight or ten warriors, with plenty of baggage. There was much talk of what materials might be used to make such a boat. Later it was learned that each boat was made from the bark of a tree not native to this region.

There were two of these boats, carrying sixteen men in all. Majestically, the craft slid upriver, paused, and angled over to land on a smooth strip of shore just below the camp. The People, cautious at first, soon began to gather at a safe distance to observe the newcomers. The wolves had followed the progress of the boats, so their arrival was not unexpected. The wolves had also attempted to describe the shape of the craft, but without success. Such a thing was so completely unfamiliar that description was difficult at best. At worst, some of the wolves had been accused of exaggeration or of outright lies.

But now, before their eyes for all to see, were the boats of the strangers. It was as the wolves had said: a long and narrow vessel that held several warriors. A couple of the men jumped from each boat into the shallow water, to drag the prow up onto the shore. The men moved very deliberately, almost slowly. White Fox had the impression that the newcomers were being very careful not to do anything unexpected. This would avoid an incident or misunderstanding of any sort.

In the front of the first canoe sat a man whose demeanor said that he was the chief, the leader of the expedition. His importance was also apparent by the fact that he wore a special tunic and leggings. The tunic was bright blue, and was crossed by bands of white as broad as a man's hand. These bands appeared to loop over the shoulders, and crossed over the chest to fasten at the waist to another such belt or strap. Where the straps crossed, they were held by a shiny metal object of some sort. His leggings or breeches were pale buff in color, much like fine buckskin.

The impressive appearance of this man's garments might suggest that he was a medicine man or holy man of some sort, but White Fox thought not. No, this man's attitude said that he was the chief of this party, no matter what his other office might be. The man wore a broad-brimmed hat as a headdress, which was adorned with a white plume of great beauty.

White Fox glanced at the other men in the boats. They all looked much alike, dressed in rough-woven cloth garments, much like he remembered among the Spanish. Most of these also wore knitted cloth caps, of varying colors. By comparison to the young chief, they had little of distinction about them. They were merely warriors, carrying out the routine tasks of this journey. He did not fail to notice, however, that several carried muskets. They could be quite dangerous, he knew from past experience. Sometimes he wished that he understood something of the medicine of these smoke poles, and how they could kill at a distance.

One of the men in the water caught his eye, and he stared in wonder. The man was wearing face-paint, and he had never known any of the outsiders, either Spanish or French, to wear face-paint. But this man had painted his face completely black, all over. Only the whites of his eyes and the snowy gleam of his teeth broke the dusky sheen that glistened on his cheeks and nose, and disappeared beneath his shirt at the neck. Then . . . *aiee*, the hands, too! Was it possible that the man had painted himself all over, for some ritual purpose? And, if so, why did he then cover his paint with garments? It would seem that he should let it show, by going naked, or nearly so. Was this a medicine man? Again, White Fox thought not. His demeanor plainly denied such status. But what . . . ?

The chief with the plumed hat now rose and stepped to shore, his right hand raised with palm forward, in the sign of peace. Fox saw that he was tall, and now he saw something else. On the man's upper lip and on his chin were small, well-shaped tufts of hair, like . . . *aiee*, like furry caterpillars! Quickly he thought to himself. The young chief of a generation ago, the one who had been called Worm-Face . . . he must have looked like this!

Now a man leaped nimbly from the other canoe to stand beside the chief. White Fox had not noticed this man before. He wore buckskins, and was obviously a native. From one of the river tribes, no doubt, acting as guide or interpreter.

"Greetings. We come in peace!" the buckskin-clad one began, in hand-signs.

Good, thought Fox. *They have someone who uses hand-signs.* This was not always true in the Southwest, when they had traded there.

"We would show our respects to your chief,"

signed the man in buckskins. "Where may we find him?"

His gaze swept the little crowd, and for a moment his eyes caught those of White Fox. There was, in passing, a recognition of sorts. The stranger had identified Fox as a holy man, and nodded slightly in verification of the fact. But that was not, at this time, his primary concern. Visitors, according to time-honored custom, should present their respects to the chief. It was pleasing to note that the strangers, or at least their guide, were familiar with the common civilities of visiting another's territory.

Now there was a stir from the direction of the camp. The crowd parted to allow the passage of a small party of delegates who advanced to meet the strangers. In the center was Yellow Bear, the real-chief, and flanking him were several band chiefs and sub-chiefs.

"Greetings," signed Yellow Bear.

"Greetings, my chief," signed the interpreter with respect. "These men are from far away. They would camp near, to learn your ways and hold council with you. This one is our chief. He has another name in his own tongue, but my people call him Blue Jacket."

The real-chief nodded.

"I am Yellow Bear," he signed. "Welcome to our camp. How are you called? Who are your people?"

"I am Lame Beaver," the other answered. "My

people are *Kenza.* We live near where the two Big Rivers meet."

"I have heard of your people," Yellow Bear observed. "Why are you with these?"

"To speak for them, until they learn to use signs better. They want to explore to the west."

The real-chief nodded again.

"Tell them they are welcome here. We are camped here for our Sun Dance."

"Yes, so I have heard. This is why we came. These men wish to find someone to guide them as they go west."

"But you . . ."

"No, no. This is the farthest west I have seen," the interpreter protested. "We need someone to go back with us to Blue Jacket's town . . ."

"His town?" signed the astonished Yellow Bear.

"Yes! They are building a town. They are bringing their women and children."

"A *town?*" Bear signed again. "For what purpose?"

"To trade! They will buy furs. Look!"

He turned and spoke to Blue Jacket, who nodded to one of the other men. That one rummaged among the packs and drew out an object which he handed to Blue Jacket. The visiting chief, in turn, removed the sheath to display a shining metal knife. There was a low gasp of approval. Since the cessation of trade with the Spanish, nothing of this sort had been seen.

"A gift, my chief," signed Lame Beaver. "They

would offer such things for trade. Also cloth, guns, and ornaments, such as these."

He pointed to a necklace on his own person, with ornaments not only of bone and stone, but strung with brightly colored beads.

"They would trade *guns?*" the real-chief asked.

"Yes," Beaver nodded eagerly. "They have been good friends to my people."

Yellow Bear nodded thoughtfully.

"Let it be so," he finally signed. "For now, let them camp with us, and we will counsel together. Tell them to camp above here. Our horses water here." He turned and pointed. "There, near the Mountain band. We will show you."

He spoke to some young men who stood near, and they motioned to the newcomers. All but a few now left the boats and began to walk to relieve tired and cramped muscles. Those still in the boats pushed off to paddle upstream to the designated camp area.

White Fox watched all this with misgivings. His memory had rushed back to his teenage years, and his father's stories of a near-fatal encounter with another party of this French tribe. It did not help at all that, as the boats pushed back out from shore, he had noticed the shiny metal seals on the packs of baggage. They were round and bore a sort of flowerlike design, which was the symbol of their tribe. He had heard his father speak of it, the *fleur-de-lis*.

But the thing that made him shiver a little, and

caused his palms to sweat, was the importance
that Red Feather always attached to this flower.
He had heard the story many times. Red Feather
had found one of these seals and picked it up,
mostly out of curiosity. It was a misunderstanding, of course, but nonetheless young Red Feather
had been shot as a thief, and barely survived.

He hoped that this contact with the same tribe
would be more pleasant.

5
>> >> >>

Shadows were long, and would soon melt together into twilight, the time White Fox loved. There was a closeness to the dusk of such an evening, a comforting warmth to the darkness. If a person were alone in the prairie twilight, it would be apparent that the world of the night creatures was coming awake. Even in the present situation, in a large camp, some of the sounds were apparent. The clatter of the grasshoppers' bright wings had given way to the chirp of their green cousins of the night. It was a pleasant sound, Fox thought.

Somewhere in the timber upstream, the hollow call of *Kookooskoos*, the great hunting owl, was answered by his mate. Closer to camp, the Little Owl, who seldom allows himself to be seen, sounded his soft whickering trill. It always reminded White Fox of the call of the raccoon, the comical ringtail who wears face-paint around his eyes. As a child, he had often imagined that these two creatures of the night were talking to each other, in the same tongue.

A distant coyote sounded his chortling bark, seeming to laugh at the amusing world in which he finds himself. From downstream, a night bird called repeatedly in the trees. There was, even farther away, the raucus booming call of a little green heron, whose voice belied his size. White Fox smiled. That small bird could be mistaken for the bellow of a distant buffalo bull.

But these night sounds were eclipsed by the sounds of the camp. The People were finishing their evening meal, and preparing for an evening of pleasant pastimes. Story-fires were lighted, and clusters of young people and those young at heart began to gather at the fires of favorite storytellers. None had started yet. In fact, some stories, such as those of the Old Man of the Shadows, must not be told until after it was fully dark. The Old Man himself had decreed it at the time of Creation.

Somewhere at the other side of camp, someone was tuning a dance drum. Tonight there would be social dancing, which would give way tomorrow to the more serious ceremonials of the Sun Dance. Tonight there would also be gambling and games. The afternoon had been spent in horse racing, and much property had changed hands in the betting. The French visitors had been quite excited over the races. The language barrier seemed to be no hindrance to their participation in the gambling.

The strangers had caused no trouble at all. They had, in fact, seemed aware at all times that proper respect for their hosts' customs was all-important. There had been some flirtation between the French and some of the eligible young women of the People, but even this had been well within the traditional limits of such contact. The visitors appeared eager to make a favorable impression, and had not approached any of the women who did not show interest.

White Fox had begun to relax, and the uneasiness he had felt was beginning to dissipate. These men surely meant no harm. But what *did* they want? Their explanation was rather vague, that of seeking a guide for their explorations. He glanced up at the approach of a figure in the dusk, and recognized Red Feather.

"*Ah-koh*, Father," he greeted. "Sit and smoke!"

Red Feather sat, after taking a stick from the fire to light his pipe. They had not yet talked of the arrival of the French. White Fox waited. It was polite to let the older man initiate the conversation. After what seemed a long time, Red Feather opened the talk with a bland question.

"Have you been to visit the camp of the French?" he asked.

"No, I . . ." stammered White Fox, confused by such an opening, ". . . I was . . . I wished to see how they behaved, first."

He felt almost like a child over this, and was

irritated with himself. Strange, that his father's stories, heard when he was small, would come back to haunt him now. Fox was actually more concerned than his father, who had been the victim of a French musket.

"Their hearts are good," assured Red Feather. "My trouble with them was a misunderstanding, and that was long ago."

"Yes, I know, Father." White Fox smiled. "But, our time in the cage in Santa Fe, and the stories of your wound . . . *aiee*, sometimes it seems any contact with outsiders brings trouble."

"I have thought much of this, Fox," Red Feather said seriously. "It is true, we have had some bad times. There is always danger, but in life there is always danger. There is also good. The benefits of trade . . . well, since Santa Fe there has been no source of knives and arrow points. It is time, maybe. And these French . . . you were too young to remember the friendships. You know your own grandfather, Woodchuck, was French?"

"Yes, Father. Sometimes I forget. I remember him as one of the People."

"Of course. But remember, Fox, the People have had only good dealings with the French. This will be good for us, you will see. *Aiee*, look at your own son, Red Horse. See how this excites him?"

Yes, thought White Fox, *he is as excited as I was, on my first trip to trade in Santa Fe*. The only trip, of course, due to the war. The People had heard that the Spanish had returned now, after a decade, and that there was no trouble. Still, because of the death and destruction the People had experienced there, no one had suggested that trade be resumed.

"Well, let us wait and see what these French want, Father."

A figure now materialized out of the dusk, and approached them, his hand raised in greeting.

"Red Feather?" the man inquired.

Fox recognized the Kenza scout from the French party.

"Yes," answered Red Feather. "Who asks?"

"Forgive me, Uncle," the Kenza replied, using hand-signs. "I use your tongue badly. May we sign?"

Red Feather nodded. "How are you called?" he asked.

"I am Lame Beaver, of the Kenzas," came the reply. "I am a wolf for the French."

"What do you seek?" asked Red Feather, puzzled.

"Your chief, Yellow Bear, sent me to you," Lame Beaver signed. "You have been to the West?"

"Yes, many times. We used to trade there."

"Good! The French chief, Blue Jacket, wants someone to go with them."

"But you . . ."

"No, no, I have never been this far west, even. You know the way."

"*Aiee!*" cried Red Feather. "That was long ago. I am an old man now. My bones ache with the weather, and with sleeping on the ground. My son, here, has taken that trail. Fox?"

"Yes," nodded Fox.

"I saw you at the river," the Kenza signed.

"True."

"You could go help them."

"No, no. I am a holy man, with duties to the People."

"It would be only a few moons," Lame Beaver countered.

"But my family . . . wife and son."

"Bring them along!"

"No, I cannot."

"Will you come and talk to Blue Jacket?"

"Why not?" Red Feather interjected into the sign-talk, speaking aloud in the tongue of the People. "Go ahead, Fox. This may be very good for the People. Good for your restless young Horse, too. Go and talk to the Blue Jacket chief, anyway."

Well, it could do no harm, Fox reasoned, to talk to their chief. He was rather intrigued, now. The Kenza wolf seemed comfortable in his relationship with the French. Maybe they were reliable. He might as well talk to them, he supposed.

"I will talk to them," he signed, a little surprised at himself.

"Good! Can you come now, holy man?"

"Maybe so. I . . ."

Their conversation was interrupted by the approach of young Red Horse. It would, indeed, be a learning experience for the boy. For a few moons . . .

"I will talk to your Blue Jacket chief," White Fox signed. "Let us go."

"Good," signed the Kenza. "Come, we will go and see him."

"What is happening?" asked Red Horse.

White Fox looked at his son, in the blossoming of youth, with the whole world to look forward to in excitement. What an adventure for the young man! Well, it might not even happen, anyway, but it would do no harm to talk of it. White Fox rose, and beckoned to his son.

"Come along, Horse. Let us go and talk to the Blue Jacket chief."

For once, Red Horse had nothing to say. Open-mouthed, he stood a moment, and then hurried after the retreating figure of White Fox.

His grandfather, still seated and enjoying his pipe, smiled knowingly and nodded. It was good, Red Feather thought to himself. It would be good for the boy, and good for the People. He had thought for several years now that the People needed something to occupy their interest. Something more, at least, than the perpetual argument about where to hold the next Sun Dance.

South Wind looked out of the lodge, and

seemed surprised to see only her father-in-law seated there.

"*Ah-koh*, Uncle. Where did my husband go?"

"To talk," he told her. "Horse is with him. They will be back soon."

"It is good," she answered, using the familiar phrase of agreement that came so easily in the tongue of the People. She disappeared inside again.

Yes, thought Red Feather, *that is true, this is good*. He wished that his age and the stiffness in his joints did not prevent him from going himself.

6
>> >> >>

The conversation was a strange one, carried on partially in French and Kenza, and translated through hand-sign talk. As nearly as White Fox could tell, Blue Jacket, the French officer, was a highly intelligent and interesting individual. At least if the Kenza was relaying the conversation accurately. He seemed sincere, anxious to enlist the help he needed, and willing to furnish payment in the form of trade goods.

"We wish to explore to the west," Blue Jacket said through the interpreter. "Can you guide us?"

"How long?" asked White Fox.

"Maybe a moon . . . two moons."

"And my family?"

"Your son? Bring him too. Your wife if you wish."

"Where do you want to go?"

"West. There is a river north of here, beyond the River of the Kenzas. We will follow it."

White Fox nodded.

"We have never been that far north, my chief. But, I do know of this river."

"Good. Then you can talk with the tribes there?"

"Yes. We know some of the Mandan tongue. And, hand-signs. But how can we speak with *you*?"

Blue Jacket's eyes opened wide with astonishment. Then he began to laugh.

"I must hurry with learning sign-talk, no?"

Lame Beaver relayed this, and the laughter was general.

"It is good," the Kenza signed. "Blue Jacket is learning rapidly."

"How is it that you are not going?"

The Kenza spread his palms and shrugged.

"It has seemed that a tribe of the prairie, such as your people, would be better. We live in towns, and have little contact with the people of the plains to the west."

It was true, reflected White Fox. There was a barrier of custom and life-style. The Kenza were growers, but each year mounted a big fall buffalo hunt out onto the plains. At times in the past, some of the purely hunting tribes had resented this incursion into their hunting grounds. Yes, he thought, if I were a Kenza I would hesitate to lead a party of outsiders into the plains.

He was still unsure of the final purpose for this expedition, and inquired again.

"To make trade," the blue-coated officer explained again through the interpreter. "We wish all tribes to bring furs . . . beaver, fox, otter . . . to our lodge to trade."

There was some confusion at this point over the fact that the hand-signs were not very specific. The signs for "lodge" or dwelling and for "town" were both used.

"What sort of lodges?" probed White Fox.

"Like ours, but different," signed the Kenza. "You will have to see with your own eyes."

The whole idea was intriguing, and Fox's natural curiosity was stirring. There were things occurring that he must see.

"When would this journey happen?" he asked.

"Soon," came the relayed reply. "Will you come back with us? The journey starts from our town."

"We cannot, until after the Sun Dance."

"Of course. You must have your ceremonies. Then we will leave."

"It is good."

White Fox and the French officer clasped hands in agreement, and Blue Jacket turned to rejoin his party.

Young Red Horse, who had been investigating the French camp, now came up beside his father.

"Father," he said quietly but insistently, "did you see the man with black face-paint?"

Fox had forgotten the man, whom he had seen earlier. He turned to look. The man was passing on the way to the fire, carrying an armful of

wood. In the darkness of evening, the reflected
light from the fires glistened on the oily darkness
of the blackened skin. The dusky one saw their
gaze and smiled, a friendly smile with even white
teeth, and passed on his way.

"Yes," Fox observed, half to himself. "I saw
him today."

He turned to Lame Beaver with the question.

"What of the man with black face-paint?" he
signed. "He is their holy man?"

"No, no," returned the Kenza, laughing. "You
have never seen a black man?"

"Of course. We paint ourselves black on returning from a hunt or war party, to show that
someone has been killed."

The Kenza laughed again, with an all-knowing
arrogance that irritated White Fox. No wonder, he
thought, that some of the plains tribes detested
these people.

"They are born with that color," the Kenza
signed.

"*Aiee!*" Fox exclaimed. "Then, it is a vow or
ceremony that the mother does?" he signed.

Lame Beaver laughed smugly. "No, his tribe is
that color."

"All of them? He is not of the French tribe?"

"Of course not. He is a captive."

Here, again, the hand-signs became confusing.
No sign exactly expressed the status of a slave, so
"captive" was as close as the interpreter could
come.

"But he does not behave as a captive," protested White Fox.

"How should a captive behave?" shrugged the other. "He was born into this, and knows no other way."

"There are *more* of them?"

"Yes. Several, at the French town."

This was very confusing. In all of Fox's experience there was no such thing. A captive was a captive. He might be killed, or released, or adopted into the captor's tribe. Some married and raised families, and in merging with their new people, were no longer captives. In a generation or two, their origins would be all but forgotten. But this . . . *aiee*, a captive tribe *within* a tribe? It was hard to grasp.

"He is like your horses," offered the interpreter.

This was even more confusing.

"But he is a man!" protested White Fox.

The Kenza merely shrugged.

Good weather held, and the Sun Dance was considered one of the best in recent years. The dances and prayers of thanksgiving for the return of the sun, the grass, and the buffalo were carried out. There were prayers of supplication, and requests for good health and success. Expressions of patriotism and valor were coupled with sacrifices and vows of penitence. The dances and chanting continued through the nights, or until the danc-

ers and those who beat the rhythms on the big
drums were exhausted. Then their places were
taken by others, and the celebration continued.

In some of the "open" dances the allies of the
People took part. The Head Splitters had done so
for generations, and now visitors from other tribes
were invited to participate. Somewhat to the surprise of the People, Blue Jacket himself stepped
into the arena of the Sun Dance lodge and into
the circle of dancers. Some of his men followed,
and it was very good. Symbolically, a friendship
between the two tribes was being solidified.

To White Fox's amazement, one of the first to
follow the French officer's example was the "captive," now called Black Paint by the People. He
had made a good impression, with his cheerful
manner and his helpfulness. This was enhanced
even more as he began to dance. The man seemed
to have an innate feel for the rhythms of the
drums. Soon sweat glistened on his dusky skin,
and he stripped off his shirt for comfort. Observ-
ers watched in admiration as Black Paint threw
himself wholeheartedly into the sinuous movements of the dance. He followed the moves of the
others, but also improvised, adding new and exciting movements. When the Guest Dance was
finished, there was a cheer of approval for the outsider.

How strange, thought Fox, this man's status. A
captive, yet allowed to participate in such a ceremony, and even cheered by the French party.

Aiee, there was much that he did not understand about this.

Finally, the ceremonies and festivities were at an end. The People began their packing for travel and their good-byes. Many families with friends or relatives in other bands exchanged children until their next meeting. A season with another band was considered a good part of a youngster's education, an opportunity for new experiences and to see new country. White Fox himself had once spent a season in the pueblo of his mother's parents. This experience in another tribe had considerably expanded his knowledge.

Now Blue Jacket seemed anxious to depart. The soldiers were packing in preparation to leave.

South Wind was very reluctant to take part in the expedition at first. Her lifelong shyness became more pronounced at such times. When she found that she was expected to sit and ride in one of the long boats, Fox thought that she would refuse entirely.

"But Red Horse and I will be with you," he told her.

"I know, but to sit in that . . . is it safe, Fox?"

"Of course. You saw all those men riding in it."

"Maybe so . . . *aiee*, Fox, I am afraid."

"And I, a little," her husband admitted, "but if we fall out, we swim to shore."

She laughed, then, and he knew that she would be all right. After all, going with her family was to be preferred to being left alone. Arrangements were made for friends to transport their lodge to the next camp of the Southern band, near the river of the Ar-kenzas this season.

''We will see you there, in two or three moons,'' White Fox called as the paddles of the boatmen dipped into the water and the canoes moved out into the current.

7

>> >> >>

The town of the French was like nothing the People had ever seen. It was smaller than White Fox had imagined, only some thirty paces on each side. It stood well up on the slope above the river-bank, a solid square of logs set in the ground on end, to form an impassable barrier. There was one entrance to the palisade, facing to the south. This seemed odd to the People, whose doorways always faced east to greet the rising of the sun. There must even be an opening at the east side of a council ring. It was a matter of religion. The idea of an enclosure with only one entrance was threatening enough, but to have the opening on the south . . . *aiee!*

The barrier formed by the log palisade was a trifle higher than a man could reach. At two of the corners, however, some sort of structure seemed to loom even higher. Looking inside, they could see that there were square lodges of logs in all four corners. Two of these rose high above the wall, small and square, with small square holes. Men's faces could be seen at these openings.

"*Aiee!*" exclaimed Red Horse. "They place one lodge on top of another!"

"Like your grandmother's people sometimes do," agreed White Fox.

"But those are of mud, Father. These are made of thick trees."

To people of the prairie, this was inconceivable. The scarcity of wood in their region made even the acquisition of lodge poles a problem sometimes. They would travel many sleeps merely to reach an area where poles for their skin lodges could be obtained. In the western reaches of their territory, the Mountain band used lodge pole pines, hardly thicker than a man's arm, but several times the height of a man. In the East, cottonwoods in the river bottoms sometimes grew in thick stands, crowding each other into tall slim growth as they competed for the sun. But nowhere among the People was there the use of large trees as logs for construction. Their nomadic life-style did not permit it, even if such timber had been available.

Red Horse watched, fascinated, as workmen plastered mud into the crevices of a structure in process of construction. Others chopped and notched logs. There would be, it appeared, four or five of the lodges inside the palisade, in addition to those against the outside walls. All seemed to be of the two-level sort.

White Fox felt the all-too-familiar trapped feeling, the dread of being enclosed without means of
escape. He had felt it even before his dreadful
experience in the Spanish jail. South Wind had
always teased him about this, but he knew that
she understood. One does not grow up in a skin
lodge without such feelings. The lodges of the
People could be pegged tightly and insulated
against winter's cold. They could also be rolled up
at the bottom, to allow the cooling breezes of
summer to blow through the dwelling. And in an
emergency, the skin lodge presented the possibility of escape in any direction, merely by slipping
under the lodge cover to roll outside. To be closed
in by logs and mud in dwellings like this was a
very threatening thing. Fox was glad that they
would not be asked to stay in these lodges. It was
summer, and as they traveled with the French exploring party, there would be no need for any but
a temporary shelter in case of bad weather.

They had become well acquainted with Blue
Jacket in the few days they had been in the canoes. The officer was trying hard to learn the
hand-signs, and was making good progress. Several of the soldiers, too, had shown an interest,
and were rapidly developing the skill. One of
those who was quickly learning to use the hand-
signs was the black man. The name given him by
the People had stuck, and to them he was Black
Paint or, more usually, merely "Paint."

Young Red Horse had been merely curious at

first, but had quickly developed a friendship with Paint. The man was friendly and cheerful but not overbearing, and perhaps represented less of a threat to a teenager than the French soldiers did. White Fox and South Wind decided that such an acquaintance could be very good for their son. He might learn much from this man of another culture.

As soon as they had arrived here at Fort de Chastaigne, the Kenza interpreter had told them good-bye and headed for his home and family. The Kenza village could be seen in the distance downstream. A heavy blue fog of cooking smoke layered out among the trees along the river, hanging over the Kenza town in the still summer evening. He seemed to have little interest in the expedition, now that his job was finished, and his communication skills were rapidly becoming unneeded.

"You can camp there," Blue Jacket signed, indicating an area just outside the wall.

"We will go a little farther," White Fox replied. "Near those trees by the river, maybe?"

"It is good," agreed Blue Jacket. "We will start in two, maybe three days."

There was time now to explore and observe the rapidly growing fort and its surroundings. In a plot near the river, a well-kept garden flourished. They could see corn and tobacco plants, as well as pumpkins and other plants which at this distance appeared to be beans.

"Father, look!" Red Horse pointed. "That island in the river—there are spotted buffalo on it!"

"Yes," White Fox chuckled. "They keep them as we keep horses and dogs. I have seen them in Santa Fe."

"*Aiee!*" exclaimed Horse. "They ride them and eat them?"

"No, no . . . well, eat them sometimes. The Spanish used them to pull carts."

"Carts?"

"Yes, a sort of pole-drag with round sections of log to make it roll . . . ah, Red Horse, you would have to see it."

"Do these people use such things?" the youngster asked in wonder.

"I do not know. Maybe. But these spotted buffalo . . . they are different. These are females . . ."

He paused, puzzled.

"Father, why are they kept on the island? How did they get there?"

"*Aiee,* I do not know, son. Ask your friend Paint, there."

He pointed to the black man who was passing by.

Instantly, Red Horse called out and ran to converse with the slave.

"Paint, tell me of the spotted buffalo on the island, there," he signed.

"Yes? What did you want to know?"

"Why are they there? How did they get there? What are they used for?"

The negro threw back his head and laughed, a melodious laugh that seemed to come from deep within him.

"One at a time," he signed in protest. "We took them there, swimming behind a boat, with a rope on their horns."

"Why?" asked the astonished Red Horse.

"To keep them from leaving. They do not like to swim."

"But . . . their use? You eat them?"

"Sometimes. But they are kept for milk."

"Milk?"

"Yes. For cooking, and for the children."

"Wait, Paint. I do not understand. You will kill one of these just for the milk in its bag?"

"No, no. Not kill it. Just take the milk. Morning and evening."

Now Red Horse was completely confused.

"But how . . ."

"Ah, you will see. Come, soon I will go over to get the milk, and you can go with me. Ask your father."

Red Horse nodded and loped off to ask permission.

He was not certain which seemed more miraculous. The squeezing of large quantities of milk into a wooden bucket was startling enough. But perhaps the greater mystery was that the animal would stand still for such a thing. She stood sleepily, calmly chewing her cud while Paint finished his task and moved on to the next cow.

Aiee, thought Red Horse. *How can I tell my friends of this? They would never believe it.*

Paint filled his buckets and the two returned to the boat for the crossing back to the fort. The cows wandered back into the island's grassy meadow.

"Why do they stay here?" Red Horse signed. "They could swim across, you said."

The black man smiled.

"They would not want to swim unless they have to."

Red Horse did not fully understand, but there were many things that he did not understand.

"Will you go west with us?" he asked on a sudden whim.

"Maybe. I am the Blue Jacket chief's man," Paint signed. "He takes me with him."

"It is good," Red Horse gestured with a smile. "My heart is good that you will come, Paint."

They arrived at the stockade, and Paint knocked at one of the finished structures. A woman came to the door and took the pails, smiling and saying something in French, apparently in thanks.

Red Horse tried not to stare. He had never seen a woman of the pale-faced outsiders before. He was struck by her beauty, but startled, not only by the paleness of her skin but by the light blue

of her eyes. For the first time he realized the reason for the name given one of the first Frenchmen
known to the People. "Sky-Eyes." Of course! The
woman's dark hair was slightly wavy, curling
around her neck and behind her ears, and Red
Horse found the unusual appearance quite exciting.

The most unusual thing about her, however,
besides the eyes, was her dress. Womanly curves
were accentuated from the waist up, by a tightly
laced bodice that lifted and separated her breasts.
From the waist down, however, the voluminous
billow of her skirts completely concealed any hint
of legs, clear to the ankles. How odd, he thought.
The women of the People were traditionally
proud of their tall build and attractive appearance. A woman's buckskin dress fell above the
knee, exhibiting a shapely expanse of leg by delib-
erate design. Why was it otherwise with the
French woman? Did she have ugly legs? Surely
not. The rest of her body suggested fine bone
structure, and surely . . . *aiee*, there were so
many new things!

He also noted that the attitude of the black
slave was quite different toward this woman.
Paint showed an exaggerated amount of respect,
bowing his head and averting his eyes as he spoke
to her.

They left the stockade, Red Horse now filled
with questions.

"Whose woman is this?" he signed.

Paint rolled his eyes and did not answer until they were well outside.

"She is the trader's woman," he answered. "You should stay away from her."

"It is custom?" Red Horse signed.

The black man chuckled.

"Yes, custom," he answered. "With that woman, it is also wise."

8
≫ ≫ ≫

In the short while at Fort de Chastaigne, Red Horse began to see something of the reasons for Paint's attitude toward the trader's wife. The pretty blue-eyed woman was fascinating to him, as a distant and unobtainable desire. Her appearance, the way she moved, her bold smile which promised much but said nothing, all were exciting.

At first the boy thought that these emotions were his alone. He soon found, however, that she affected all of the men in this way. Her beauty impressed the soldiers, the employees of the trader, and the occasional rough-looking characters who hung around the fort. The latter group were referred to by the other French as *voyageurs*. Paint explained, within the limitations of hand-sign talk, that this word meant "travelers" in their tongue, but that more was implied. These were adventurers, hunters of wealth, and frequently not to be trusted.

"Do not leave your things lying around," Paint advised.

"But what is their purpose?" Red Horse pressed on.

"To the soldiers? None."

"To the trader, then?"

"No, no. They are of no help to anyone except themselves."

"Ah, yes," mused Red Horse, indicating that he understood, which in truth he did not.

The presence of the voyageurs seemed a nuisance to the trader, because of their questionable dealings with the natives. For the same reason, they were resented by the troops assigned to the trader for protection.

"Why does the Blue Jacket chief not send these men away?" asked Red Horse.

Paint shrugged. "They might be useful in a fight."

Ah, so that was it. If, in their exploration, the French party came in contact with warlike people, the voyageurs would increase fighting strength. It was odd, the soldiers and the adventurers disliking and distrusting each other, but depending on each other for protection.

On the other hand, Horse thought to himself, this situation was not entirely unknown to his own people. On occasion, it was prudent to become allies with warriors who might be disliked or distrusted, to increase fighting strength. It was exactly this sort of alliance that had embroiled

the People in the war in Santa Fe. He had heard
that story from his father and grandfather, many
times.

His thoughts reverted again to the pretty wife
of LaFontaine, the trader. She was so different. He
had never seen such a woman, and merely looking at her or even thinking of her made the man-
hood stir within him. He had felt these changes
taking place for several moons now. His feelings
toward the young women who had shared his education in the Rabbit Society had changed. This
had happened at about the time he had sprouted a
growth of fine hair along his upper lip and along
the jaw. And, of course, near his private parts.

Formerly, the girls had been merely friends,
participating in the instruction of the Rabbit Society. Athletics, use of weapons, the dance. They
had competed together in all these things. Some
had been superior at swimming, others at something else, but it had had nothing to do with girls
or boys. Until, of course, the last year or two.
Some of the girls had blossomed early, their
changes in shape pushing softly rounded curves
against the soft buckskin of their garments. It had
changed their attitude, too. There was a smug
feeling of superiority in evidence on the part of
those who graduated to the menstrual lodge for
the first time. These girls began to think in terms
of a lodge of their own. The young men's attitude
toward them changed too. Instead of companions

in the games and contests of the Rabbit Society, the girls were now potential mates.

Red Horse had been keenly aware of all this. One of his friends, Blue Swallow, was a lanky young woman who had been a companion since childhood. She had gone through this transformation in the past year. Her quick smile was now somewhat flirtatious. Horse had become almost frightened at the quick changes he saw, not only in her body but in her attitude. Swallow had always been a tease, but her playful teasing now had taken on suggestive overtones.

On the evening before Horse and his parents had left the Sun Dance with the French, she had approached in a sad but friendly manner.

"I will miss you this season, Horse," Swallow said quietly. "When will you rejoin the band?"

"I do not know," Red Horse mumbled self-consciously. "When our journey is finished."

"May your journey be safe," she said seriously. "I will look for you this autumn."

She reached for his hand, a bit clumsily, gave it a gentle squeeze, and turned quickly. In a moment she was gone, moving gracefully through the twilight toward her parents' lodge. Many times since, Horse had remembered his last sight of her, the graceful swing of her hips and the shape of her legs as she walked away from him.

The trader's wife was so very different to look at. It was odd, Horse thought, how both had stirred the maleness in him, and in such different ways.

He wondered some about the warning that the dusky Paint had voiced on that first day. To some extent, he understood. There was a woman in the Eastern band about whom there were whispered tales and ribald jokes. She had once been quite pretty, it appeared, but now carried a long scar across her left cheek, from the temple to the chin. She had long had a reputation for loose morals, and it was said that her husband had inflicted the wound when he caught her rutting with another man. The boys in the Rabbit Society had whispered and giggled about it.

Paint's suggestion about the trader's wife was that she, too, was this sort of a woman. But surely not, thought Red Horse. So pretty, so friendly, such a pure and unspoiled appearance, like that of a newly opened flower in the Moon of Roses, still touched by the morning's dew. *Aiee*, such strange new feelings bothered him when he thought of such things.

Blue Jacket was learning sign-talk quite rapidly, and seemed to enjoy the new skill. He spent part of each day with White Fox, practicing, acquiring new signs, and explaining their purpose in the exploration, that of expansion of the fur trade. The French were not particularly interested in fur trapping themselves. Their interest lay in trading, exchanging metal tools and implements, glass beads, cloth, and blankets for the furs trapped by the natives. A few of the voyageurs trapped on their own, but were usually content to carry on a somewhat questionable trade directly with the native trappers. It was apparent that to Blue Jacket these voyageurs were at best a nuisance. At worst, it seemed, they might be a threat to the entire operation, even to the establishment of the fort itself. It was not anything that Blue Jacket actually said, but his attitude. A concerned look, a frown, when the topic arose during the hand-sign lessons.

Red Horse usually watched these lessons, fascinated by the words of French that fell his way. Between this and his contact with the black slave, the young man was rapidly acquiring a few words and phrases. He would experiment with their use when conversing with Paint, who gleefully encouraged him.

Meanwhile preparations continued for the proposed journey. It was four days, not three, before all was ready to depart. It had been decided that it would be wise to carry a quantity of trade goods to introduce to the tribes upstream. At this point the trader, too, decided to go along. This led to some reorganization, and the inclusion of a couple of the trader's employees to handle the packs.

Red Horse, when he heard of this development, was intrigued by a thought.

"Will the trader's woman go along too?" he asked Paint.

The negro rolled his eyes apprehensively.

"No, no," he said cautiously. "She will stay here."

Horse thought about that for a moment. Except for his own mother, there would be no women on the expedition.

"The French do not take women on such a quest?" he asked.

"No. Not commonly. Sometimes. But, that one! She would be a great misfortune to have along."

"But why?"

The dark man shrugged.

"She would distract the men. They would argue."

"But, Paint, she belongs to LaFontaine."

Paint nodded.

"Yes, but does she know that?" He chuckled quietly. "She does not behave so, and this upsets men. Even now, we talk of her, no?"

He paused a moment and smiled.

"We should not even talk of it," he continued. "A woman such as this makes trouble."

Red Horse could not see how such an attractive and cheerful person could cause such concern.

"But how . . . why . . ."

"She would be trouble on the journey," Paint observed, "but even more at home, maybe."

"What do you mean?" asked Red Horse.

"Think," the negro said quietly. "While her man is gone, what will she be doing?"

Horse considered this, and was still pondering when Paint spoke again.

"With a woman like this, a husband should not leave her alone."

9
>> >> >>

White Fox sat in the big canoe and watched the shore slip silently past. He was puzzled. He had assumed that the French exploring party wished to go west, and they were moving almost due north. Ah, well, they seemed to know what they wanted. At one point he casually asked the black man about it, in hand-signs.

"Why do we go north?"

Paint shrugged his shoulders.

"The river goes this way."

It was true, of course. If one travels by boat, he must follow the river. Perhaps it would flow east and west, farther upstream. This *Miss-ouree* was a large river, and especially impressive to the people from the prairie. It must be two long bow shots wide at this point, judging by the apparent size of the great sycamores on the far shore. It was difficult to estimate distance, he noticed, while sitting in the water. *Aiee*, this was no proper way to travel! How much better to sit on a fine horse.

Paint interrupted his thoughts.

"There is a smaller river that joins this from the west. It is that one we follow," he signed.

Fox nodded. This river travel was a new way, and required much learning. He turned to look at South Wind. She smiled, enjoying the excitement of the experience.

Red Horse, sitting near the front of the other canoe, was so impressed that for once he was almost speechless. Occasionally he would look across at his father, eyes wide with wonder, and point excitedly to some new or amazing sight on the shore. A deer, stepping daintily down to the river to drink, raised her head to stare at the travelers. Her spotted fawn did not even bother to look up.

A blue heron, wading in the shallows near the shore, was disturbed by their approach. The bird spread its great wings, as wide as a man's arms could reach, and rose clumsily above the water to beat its way into the air. Once airborne, every motion was smooth, majestic, and apparently effortless. The bird did not appear frightened, merely annoyed at the intrusion, and hastened to remove itself from the area.

A little farther upstream, they noticed more of the herons, perched in the trees on the shore. There seemed to be dozens, maybe hundreds of the birds, watching from the treetops and protesting the intrusion with raucous cries.

"Look, Father," Red Horse called, "this is their village. See, all the heron lodges in the trees?"

It was true. For some distance up and down the river, the massive nests of sticks were seen in any tree large enough to bear the weight. Each nest appeared to contain more wood than a person could carry. In some of the nests, the long necks and pointed beaks of young birds could be seen as they poked their heads up for a better look.

It was a unique experience for the prairie dwellers. They were familiar with the great blue herons, of course, but not in such numbers. There might be a pair or two, nesting near the People's summer camp, but the available fishing spots, as well as timber for nesting sites, limited the birds' range. Certainly a rookery of this size was an unknown thing.

On the second day of travel they approached the mouth of a sizeable stream, entering the river from the west. Blue Jacket indicated that this was their course. The canoes turned and made their way into the mouth of this stream. White Fox felt better about the situation now, somehow. They were heading west, which he had thought to be the main purpose of the expedition.

As they rounded the corner of land, a cluster of lodges appeared on the south shore. They were rectangular, made of poles and roofed with a thatch of grass or reeds.

"Mandans," observed White Fox, in answer to

a questioning look from Blue Jacket. "You wish to stop?"

"A short while," answered the officer. "Then we move on."

People from the village came running to the water to greet the newcomers, a friendly and curious crowd. The boatmen drew the canoes to shore near a number of the Mandans' round bull-boats. These were drawn up on the bank and over-turned, apparently to avoid gathering rainwater.

The general attitude was friendly but cautious. By previous agreement, White Fox initiated the dialogue.

"Greetings, my brothers," he signed. "I am White Fox, of the Elk-dog People to the south. I talk for these." He indicated Blue Jacket and the trader, and then the rest of the party with a sweep of his hand.

"Who are they? How are they called?" signed a man who seemed to carry himself with authority.

"They come from far away, my chief. They wish to trade."

Carefully, he lifted the metal knife from his waist.

"See? Weapons, tools like this, for furs."

There was a murmur in the crowd. The possibility of such trading was impressive.

"Why do you speak for them?" asked the Mandan suspiciously.

"They are only learning hand-signs," explained Fox. "We are known on the prairie, and we teach them as we go. They would hold council with you, and give gifts."

The Mandan nodded.

"It is good. We know of your Elk-dog People, and they are respected. Come, we will hold council."

He led the way to a somewhat larger lodge which appeared to be a meeting place. Since the weather was warm, however, the council would be held outside. Leaders of the village arrayed themselves on one side of the fire, and the French party on the other. A fire was mandatory in such a meeting, not for warmth or cooking, but for council. The fire would create the proper mood, to attune the spirits of the place with those of the participants.

The meeting went well. Only a few Mandan words and phrases were known to White Fox, but hand-signs served well. The hosts were impressed with Blue Jacket's halting attempts to learn. La-Fontaine distributed small gifts, such as mirrors, beads, and knives for the community's leaders. For the principal chief there was a brightly woven blanket.

"Such things can be gotten in trade for skins," White Fox explained.

The Mandans seemed greatly impressed, and promised to trap diligently in the coming fur season.

"Their town is near that of the Kenzas, where

the Big Rivers meet,'' Fox explained. ''Come there with your furs.''

There was a gnawing doubt in his mind. Would this make too great a change in the ways of such a tribe? He shrugged it aside. Of course not. Had the People not trapped for the trade in Santa Fe for a generation? But then, that trade had been destroyed by the pueblo war. Ah, well, no matter.

The Mandans wished for the visitors to stay, but Blue Jacket wanted to push on. The day was still young. There was another Mandan town two days' travel upstream, they had been told, a larger town. The trading party would plan to spend a night there, and inquire about towns farther west.

It was two days later that the People witnessed the use of the muskets carried by the French. As the canoes glided upriver, a large buck deer, his new antlers budding with the new season's growth, stood watching on shore. Blue Jacket signed for quiet, and spoke softly to one of the musketeers. Smoothly, the soldier primed the pan, leveled the weapon, and fired. The buck gave one long leap and fell kicking.

White Fox had seen and heard gunfire before, but it was a new and terrifying experience for both South Wind and young Red Horse. The buck had been well over a bow shot away, and had been struck down so effortlessly! And the flash, noise, and smoke . . . *aiee*, it had been like a spear of real-fire, hurled at the earth by Rain

Maker in the Moon of Thunder. Red Horse coughed at the lungful of acrid white smoke that came drifting past.

The canoe shot forward toward the shore, and the deer was quickly dressed out.

"We camp here," Blue Jacket signed. "Tonight we have fresh meat!"

There was much laughter and merriment among the soldiers as they prepared to camp, but Red Horse approached his father with concern.

"Father, they do not make the apology?"

White Fox shook his head, a little sadly. Among the People, a significant kill, such as the first buffalo kill of the season, demanded some ceremony. An acknowledgement, a statement to the deceased animal.

My brother, we are sorry to kill you, but your flesh is our life, as the grass is yours. May your people prosper . . .

Then the celebration could take place, the joy and the feasting. But here, there had been no apology.

"No," said White Fox, "that is not their way."

There was another, unspoken observation by young Red Horse. It was the same thought that made the palms of his father damp with nervous sweat, remembering Santa Fe. It was all too apparent that the death-dealing medicine of the smoke pole, the musket, could reach farther than a bow shot. Equally apparent, it could strike a man as easily as it had the deer on the shore.

*   *   *

The land and the river seemed to flatten out as
they traveled westward. The rolling hills gave
way to a sameness, the flat, level plain on either
side of the river stretching in both directions until it met a distant rise of ground. There was less
vegetation too, only the short prairie grass, and
the fringe of willows along the streams. Twice it
was necessary to get out of the boats and drag
them by hand across a shallow riffle.

They had stopped at several towns now, both
Mandan and Pawnee. They had been well received, and there was much interest in the potential of fur trade. But, for the past ten sleeps, there
had been little change in the appearance of the
land. Each village told of another, farther upstream, and they traveled on. White Fox was becoming concerned. How far would Blue Jacket
wish to go? And, would there not be a limit to
how far it would be practical to trade? Fox could
see no end to this flat land with the river slicing
through it. In addition, the dry season, the Red
Moon of summer, was nearing. If the river dried
up, they would be on foot.

10

>> >> >>

Captain LeFever was increasingly concerned.
He could see that the stream became smaller each
day. It concerned him that he did not know the
climate of the region. It might be that this was an
unusual year, somewhat drier than usual. On the
other hand, he had noted that the land appeared
progressively less green as they moved west. This
present area was obviously a region of less rainfall, perhaps by half, than the locale of the fort.
Someone must study this phenomenon someday.

He thought of the vast difference in the plants
of this upriver landscape. Botany had been an interest to him as a student, and the vast richness of
undocumented species in the interior of this continent had boggled his mind. They had cut great
trees to build the fort and the palisade. Hard-
woods grew in great numbers there. There were
oaks of several species, mostly strange to him. A
type of walnut, with dark, purplish heartwood,
and several other species that bore nuts. There

were sycamores, a less desirable species for construction, but beautiful in their form and growth. If anything, he thought the sycamores more beautiful than those of home. Where the bark of the European variety was yellowish to pale green, those of New France appeared chalky white, a startling appearance in a dark forest.

He had looked forward in eager excitement to this assignment. The romance, the adventure of establishing a new post at the junction of two of the great rivers of the West. He would be at the very forefront, the cutting edge, of exploration of the continent.

Things had been changing rapidly, even in his lifetime. The competition with the English, which had once seemed so important, had cooled somewhat in recent years. There was no formal agreement, as far as he knew. The French had traditionally kept to the north, and the English to the south, as both penetrated westward across the continent. But now the westward push of the English had slowed. There seemed little competition, particularly in the Far West, along the great river that the natives called the *Miss-iss-ippi*. France had pushed outposts to the Great Lakes, then on to the west. There were tales of shining mountains and wide skies, and of Spanish settlements to the southwest.

There had been the theory of a northwest water passage to the western ocean, and hence to India. Some still sought such a waterway, encouraged by the chain of the Great Lakes, stretching across the continent. A less popular theory postulated a *southwest* passage, but this idea, too, was cooling in its enthusiasm. LeFever, along with others on the frontier, was already realizing that the important factor for commerce was not a passage *through* the continent, but the continent itself.

Consequently, he was thrilled with the assignment to build a western outpost. The farthest west outpost on the entire continent, in fact. What a challenge! The opening of virgin territory, the blazing of new trails.

It had been a mixed blessing. The assignment was basically to build a trading post, so that the trader, LaFontaine, could ply his vocation. The trader had been awarded the franchise for the district, for what reason LeFever did not know. Such privileges were given to repay political debts, or to relatives of noble families, without apparent reason. There was a deeply buried spark of resentment that smouldered within the captain's innermost soul. He resented the system a little bit, though he had clawed his way upward successfully within it. He disliked the trader to some extent, and not only because of the trading franchise which seemed undeserved. The man was indecisive, and unappreciative for the assistance that the military was furnishing. Ah, well, the assignment was to help him, and LeFever would do so. Actually, their establishment of trading contacts on this expedition had been quite successful.

But there was the other part of his mission, known to practically no one at Fort de Chastaigne except the captain. He was to try to establish contact with Spain, to the southwest. There was a settlement there, it was said, centuries old, called Santa Fe. To set up international trade with Spain, across the continent, before the English realized what was happening, would greatly solidify French ownership of the land. This was LeFever's semi-secret mission, and the one which drove him westward with enthusiasm.

He had managed to learn from the neighboring Kenzas that the place did exist, and that the tribes of the plains did trade there. There had apparently been a war with the natives a few years before, but that was resolved now, it was said. Spain had returned to Santa Fe and the situation was calm. They had been fortunate to find people of the plains who had actually been there. This White Fox, who was a priest or holy man of some sort, seemed to be a highly intelligent man. LeFever wondered if White Fox had realized that there must be another purpose to this journey. It was painfully obvious, at least to LeFever, that White Fox and his family were not really needed as interpreters. LeFever was already using the hand-signs well. Soon he would have to speak with White Fox about the secondary mission. It was apparent that the stream would not carry the canoes much farther, and if it became much smaller, as the summer's heat increased, it might even be difficult to return.

There was one other worry in the back of LeFever's mind. As if he did not have enough problems, there had been the matter of the voyageurs. Originally civilian employees and mercenaries on the frontier, some of these soldiers of fortune had, when their term of employment ran out, chosen to stay as privateers. There was little that could be done about it. They traded directly with the natives, sometimes unfairly, and interfered with the legitimate trade sanctioned by the Crown. To make matters even worse, as French subjects such freebooters were entitled to the protection of the Crown, and it was LeFever's duty to provide it. This rankled within him, even more than his dislike of the trader with whom he must work.

The worst of the lot was a disreputable sort who went by the name of Baptiste DuBois. Despite LeFever's warnings, he had been establishing trade of his own around Fort de Chastaigne, undercutting the authority of the outpost. The captain had sometimes wondered if DuBois and LaFontaine might in some way be associated, but he could see no way that it could benefit the trader. He knew, but could not prove, that DuBois had traded brandy to the natives, and worse, to the soldiers as well. If there was anything that could destroy such an outpost on the frontier more quickly than drunkenness, he could not imagine what it would be.

It bothered him considerably to be absent from the fort for this long. He was not concerned about the natives. They had had excellent relations with the nearby Kenzas. His chain of command was strong, and construction of the buildings would continue. But there was some concern about the four families who lived at the fort. True, they did lend a stabilizing influence, and make the frontier seem more like home. In fact, next year, perhaps, he might bring Collette, his intended bride. Ah, it had been so long . . . It did not help his hunger to have the flirtatious wife of the trader at the fort. She seemed to flaunt her availability at every opportunity. It was difficult to understand how, or why, such a woman would be wedded to the taciturn trader. Since the first day of her arrival, she had tortured the loins of every man at the post with her hints and implied promises. LeFever was certain that with little effort he could establish an affair with her himself. He had so far resisted all of her broad invitations. That would be most unwise, and could jeopardize the entire mission. Still, he rankled at the thought of such a lovely creature bedding with a man he disliked and distrusted as much as Jacque LaFontaine.

Ah, life is difficult, he was forced to admit. Even this, the most exciting of all the assignments he had ever had, was fraught with problems.

More problems, perhaps, than he had ever had. Could it be, he wondered, that this is the way life is? Does a situation have problems in direct proportion to its desirability? It seemed entirely possible.

The soldiers were starting campfires, as shadows lengthened. They were tired. Four times today they had stopped to lighten the loads of the big canoes so that they could half drag, half float them across a sandy riffle. It was time to do something. If they turned back now, they could retrace their path with little difficulty. If they lingered in this arid country, it was highly questionable whether, in a week, or even in a day or two, they could float the canoes downstream.

He had thought that surely by this time they would have seen the mountains that would be their landmark, where they would turn to go to the Spanish settlements. Perhaps he had been foolish, not to confide earlier in White Fox and find out what was happening. Yes, that had long been a fault of his, the need to do it all himself.

Self-sufficiency had been a major part of his success. It had been a necessity, in fact, as he rose from humble beginnings to a military career. But, he was just starting to realize, there are some things that one simply cannot handle alone. Like the exploration of a continent, perhaps.

He rose to seek White Fox.

11
>> >> >>

Night was falling on the river that the soldiers had begun to call the "Platte." Shadows grew longer, such as they were. The country was largely without notable landmarks except for the river on which they traveled, and the low rolling land in the distance to the north and south. There was very little to cast a shadow. The river still became smaller as they progressed upstream.

White Fox had spent enough time in the western portion of the People's range to know the behavior of its rivers. He supposed that this area would be much the same. In the summer, the streams narrowed to a trickle, or even to a series of water holes along their courses. There was water beneath, and it could be obtained for drinking by digging in the sand. There would, however, not be enough to float even a small bull-boat, much less the big canoes of the French. There was a saying among the People, that in these regions the rivers run upside down in the summer. The sandy bed was visible at the surface, and the water hidden beneath the ground.

White Fox was increasingly concerned over their need to return. It must be before the river receded to a seasonal low point which would prevent use of the boats. Yes, he decided with a sigh, tonight he must speak to Blue Jacket. He did not understand the officer's attitude. The towns of the Mandans, and even of the Pawnees, had become scarcer. This was not trapping country. Their mission to explore and contact potential fur traders seemed to have been accomplished. Why, then, did Blue Jacket push on?

The French officer had made much progress in sign-talk, and Fox often felt that his function as an interpreter was totally unneeded. Sometimes he wondered why he had been asked to join this expedition at all. There seemed no real purpose in it, and that made him uneasy because he did not understand. Yes, he would consult with Blue Jacket. That, at least, was increasingly easy. The officer had not only proven adept at hand signs, but had been willing to learn some of the Mandan tongue. This allowed White Fox to also expand his use of Mandan.

In addition to all this, it was impossible to be with the French all of the time every day without picking up words and phrases. Red Horse, in particular, was chattering in French quite easily now, aided by the black man.

Fox had just decided to go and seek Blue Jacket

for the conversation he felt necessary, when he saw the officer approaching. Blue Jacket signed a greeting, and then spoke, using his own tongue.

"My friend, may we talk?"

"Of course."

"Come, let us walk."

He led the way out of the camp area next to the river, and the two strolled in the twilight. The air was cooling rapidly, and as always, there were sounds of the night creatures coming awake to replace the sounds of the day. There was a hollow cry which Fox believed to be that of the small owl who lives in the ground. A curious creature, that one, not found in his own tall-grass country. A coyote called in the distance, and Fox smiled to himself. That, at least, was always the same.

Blue Jacket stopped, and stood looking back at the twinkling fires of the night camp. They were necessarily small, due to the scarcity of fuel. The People had taught the others, many sleeps ago, how to use dried buffalo dung to supplement the available sticks from scrubby willows along the stream.

"Fox," said the officer at last, "we must plan."

White Fox nodded, and waited. Maybe now he would learn something of whatever it was that was driving Blue Jacket onward to the west.

"I must ask you," Blue Jacket went on, "how far to the mountains?"

"The *mountains?*"

"Yes, how far . . . how many sleeps?"

White Fox was totally unprepared for this inquiry. Why did Blue Jacket want to know this?

"I do not know," he admitted. "What . . ."

The officer stopped the question with a wave of his hand.

"But you have been to Santa Fe, no?" he asked.

"Yes, the People used to trade there, before their war."

"And you were there?"

"Yes, with our last trading party."

"So I was told."

"But, I do not understand," Fox protested. "What has this to do with your fur trade?"

Blue Jacket hesitated for a few moments, pacing nervously a step or two. Then he answered, in a mixture of hand-signs, French, and a few words of Mandan.

"This party has two purposes," he said simply. "One is the fur trade. The other is to find the way to the Spanish settlement in Santa Fe."

"But *monsieur*, this is not the way!"

Blue Jacket stared for a moment.

"I have been told to go west to the mountains, and then south to Santa Fe. This is not correct?"

"No . . . well, yes, *monsieur*, but not here . . . no, much farther south."

White Fox now understood why the French officer had felt the need to push on. He was trying to reach a goal that had not been clearly stated. *Aiee*, if they had only known . . .

"I have heard 'follow the river west,'" Blue Jacket was saying.

"But not this river!" Fox explained. "*Aiee*, it would be better by land, also."

"By land?"

"Yes, with horses. It is unfortunate, that we did not know what you wanted."

"Wait . . . with horses?"

"Yes, we could supply horses, and take you there."

"How long . . . how many sleeps?"

White Fox considered a moment.

"From your town, a moon's time. Maybe a little more."

"You would follow the other river? The Kenza?"

"No, no, the Ar-kenza. A few sleeps overland to reach it, at first."

Blue Jacket seemed very serious, and somewhat depressed.

"We have wasted much effort," he said finally.

White Fox was still not certain why it was so important to reach Santa Fe.

"You wish to go there this season?" he asked.

"I had hoped for that," Blue Jacket replied.

"It might be done," suggested Fox. "We would need to return quickly, and begin again."

Blue Jacket smiled ruefully.

"At least the trading part has gone well. I should have . . . Ah, Fox, if I had known you as I do now, I would have told you what we seek."

A strange statement, thought White Fox. The ways of outsiders were strange indeed. Now, because Blue Jacket had not told what he really sought, he may have thrown away the season. Fox was not certain whether there would be time to return to the fort, obtain new supplies and horses, and start out again, this time on the old Southwest Trail. He wondered where the Eastern band had camped for the summer, and if they would have horses to trade. The Eastern band would be the nearest, and consequently the quickest, source of horses.

White Fox was also wondering whether he really wanted to guide the French party to Santa Fe. It would be a hard, hurried journey. Even at best, the party might not be able to return before the snows fell. At worst, if there happened an early winter, it might be necessary to winter with the Red Rocks band, or even with their Head Splitter allies.

Ah, well, it could be decided later. The important thing now was to retrace their journey, back down the river before it dwindled away.

Blue Jacket interrupted his thoughts.

"We should start back in the morning, no?"

White Fox nodded.

"Yes, it would be wise."

"Come, then, I will tell the others."

Blue Jacket wasted no time. No sooner had they reached the camp than he shouted to call everyone together. The soldiers straggled in from their scattered fires, curious as to what might be the cause of the assembly.

The officer waited until all had gathered, and then began to speak. He used French, but most of the announcement could be understood by White Fox. It is far easier, Fox reflected, to understand an unfamiliar tongue than to speak it.

"The expedition has been a success," Blue Jacket was saying. "We have established trade with many people, for the coming fur season."

There was a slight murmur of agreement and approval.

"Now," Blue Jacket continued, "there is a second purpose to this mission."

Another murmur told White Fox that this had been unknown to the boatmen-soldiers.

"We are to find a suitable trail to the Spanish settlement of Santa Fe."

This time the murmur was louder and more intense. The evening air seemed tense with the excitement of this new information.

"We have learned," Blue Jacket continued, "of another way, a shorter trail. However, we will need horses. So, we will return toward Fort de Chastaigne, at least partway. Tomorrow, we start back downriver."

There was a pleased murmur of surprise, and the men drifted away, talking excitedly.

Fox smiled to himself. Blue Jacket was a good leader. It had been apparent, outside the camp in the twilight, that the officer was disappointed and distressed at his newfound knowledge. At the council a short while later, none of this was apparent. Blue Jacket had made the disappointment sound like an exciting new discovery. His men were excited and pleased.

Yes, a good leader.

12

>> >> >>

Red Horse was pleased at the announcement that they would be turning back. There was, in the back of his mind, the thought of a Mandan girl who had smiled at him in one of the towns along the river. Several had done so, because he was a handsome young man. But this was a special smile, a smile that held a great deal of promise. In addition, he could not avoid the fact that this Mandan girl reminded him greatly of Swallow, back at home among the People.

It was not entirely that she looked like Swallow, but her mannerisms, her movements, the shape of her legs and the swing of her hips as she walked. He was very powerfully attracted to her. Several times, during the evening that they had spent in her village, she had been quite obvious in her approach. A promising smile, an arching lift of the eyebrow, and the broad hint that she would not be displeased if Red Horse sought more of her company. He had thought to do so, but by the time he had mustered the courage, it was too late. She was nowhere to be found, and he sought his sleeping robes in frustration. The opportunity to share some time with the girl with the inviting smile had come and gone, while he still tried to decide whether it was real.

He had seen her the next morning as they prepared to continue their journey. She smiled at him, and again he was charmed, but it was not the same. There was no promise. There could not be, because he was leaving, and quite likely he would never see her again. He felt a sadness at the lost opportunity as their glances met, and he thought he saw a hint of the same sadness in her eyes.

And now they were turning back. It took only a short while for Red Horse to realize that, in turning back, they would retrace their journey back downriver. For some time it had seemed that they might need to leave the stream and continue overland. To turn back instead would probably mean night stops in each town they had visited on the outward journey. That, in turn, hinted to him that they might spend a night with the Mandans in the village of the young woman who had so impressed him. "Girl-Who-Smiled," he had begun to call her in his mind. It would be good to see her again. This time, he told himself, he would be able to see the situation more quickly, and react appropriately.

There were major flaws in all this. He did not

know the girl's real name, or even the name of
her village. In fact, he was not certain how many
days' journey downstream it might be. But the
decision by Blue Jacket had given him a thrill of
excitement, and the possibility of adventure.

Flights of fancy carried him in his imagination
to far-out situations. There was no reason, for instance, why one of the People should not marry
outside the tribe. Both Sky-Eyes and, yes, Woodchuck, his own great-grandfather, had been outsiders. French, in fact, who had joined the People.
There were other examples which came to mind.
Aiee, he had almost forgotten! His grandfather,
Red Feather, had done so too, marrying Moon
Flower, daughter of an elder of the pueblo people.
Strange, he thought. He had never thought of his
grandmother as an outsider, even after visits to
the pueblo of her people. He wondered if this had
been an exciting romance for his grandparents,
long ago. Probably not as exciting as he visualized
his own pending romance. But no matter. There
was still much precedent for marriage to outsiders.

This line of thought, along with the continued
fleeting ideas of romance and adventure stimu-
lated him. The almost-forbidden ecstasies of an
exotic experience with the unknown kept him excited. He could imagine the looks on the faces of
his friends when he returned from this great summer of exploration with an adoring wife. One of
exceptional beauty, too. He could hardly wait to

see her again, and wondered what her name might actually be. Not that there was anything inaccurate about "Girl-Who-Smiled," but she might already have a name that she preferred. He would ask her.

The days of travel passed slowly. Apparently they had turned back none too soon. It was necessary to unload more frequently than on the upstream journey. Some places where they had floated the empty canoes over shallows by wading and pulling were now too shallow even for that. It was necessary to lift and carry. "Portage," the soldiers called it.

Even so, they seemed to catch up with the receding river in a few days, and the going was better. The river was large enough here to assure that if they kept going they would not be stranded in a dry riverbed.

Red Horse continued to relate well to Paint, the black man. Their language difference became progressively less important, as Horse picked up more words of French, and the negro became more proficient in hand-signs. Their conversations consisted of an odd mix of sign-talk, French, and the People's tongue, with a few words of Mandan.

They passed the first of the Pawnee and Mandan towns they had visited on the outgoing journey, pausing only briefly. At one they stayed overnight. Red Horse thought that they must be nearing the village of Girl-Who-Smiled, and ventured to inquire.

"Paint," he asked, "was there not a larger Mandan town somewhere near here?"

The black man looked at him with a twinkle in his eye.

"You mean where the girl lived?"

Aiee, thought Horse, was it that obvious, his preoccupation with the smiling girl? He was embarrassed, and Paint continued to tease him gently.

"You do not have girls in your tribe?" he asked in mock seriousness.

"Of course!" Red Feather blurted, "but, I . . . well . . ."

He paused in confusion, and his friend chuckled.

"No matter," Paint assured him. "I know. There are few girls here, no?"

"Yes . . . no . . . I mean, that is true," mumbled Horse.

"Do you have a special woman at home?" asked the negro.

Red Horse thought for a moment.

"No," he said slowly. "There is one who is only a friend. Her name is Swallow. I do not think of her in this way."

"Like the smiling one at the Mandan town?" Paint teased again, the twinkle of mischief returning.

"No, not the same," Horse agreed.

How could Paint know his feelings? The black man had obviously noticed the same girl. Did he feel attracted to her too? Another thought occurred.

"Paint, do you have a woman?"

"Oh, yes. At the fort. A good woman."

Horse thought for a moment.

"She is black too, like you?"

He had noticed a dark woman or two at the fort, but this question had not occurred to him.

Now, Paint's eyes became wide with an expression very like that of alarm. Then he relaxed and smiled.

"Of course. It is always so," he stated.

Red Horse was quite confused. Why "of course"? Was this something one did not speak of? Ah, maybe . . . Could this have something to do with Paint's status as a lifelong prisoner?

"Is she a prisoner too?" he blurted.

The problem of translation again intervened, but finally Paint understood. He nodded.

"Yes . . . of course . . . prisoner."

"You can only have a woman who is a prisoner, then?"

Again, the negro's eyes widened with something like alarm. He became very serious.

"Red Horse, these are things that one does not talk about. Even to think . . . well, do not speak of it."

"But, Paint . . . could you take a Mandan wife?"

Paint looked puzzled for a moment and then chuckled softly.

"Maybe so, but there would be problems. Many problems. No, Horse, these are not things to talk about. Forget about it."

He paused a moment, and continued.

"Now you . . ." The twinkle in Paint's eye was back. "*You* could take a Mandan woman. Was that what you wanted?"

Horse was confused and embarrassed. He flushed hotly.

"I . . . I don't know, Paint. But there was this girl . . ."

"Yes, I saw her. Much woman, no?"

How could Paint know which girl? Well, she was certainly one who would catch the eye of any man. It was only natural that she would be noticed. Still, Horse found that he resented slightly the fact that another man, even his friend, would know his feelings, and have similar feelings himself. It nearly spoiled the anticipation.

But not quite. No, Horse decided, there were feelings in him that no one could know. And surely, no one else could understand the depth of the smile that the girl had offered him. No, there *was* something special. Well, he would speak no more of it. He did not want anyone inside his head on this matter. He would speak no more.

Paint, however, was not quite finished with the subject.

"There are many kinds of women," he observed.

Horse was confused again.

"You mean colors?"

"No, no, Horse. Well, that too, but no, I meant *kinds*."

"I do not understand."

"Some women are to marry, some can be friends, some are none of these. Some are just women. Some good, some bad . . ."

"Paint, I do not know what you are talking about."

The black man shrugged.

"I do not either. No matter. It is something a man will not understand until later."

"Later?"

"Yes, Horse," Paint said, a little sadly. "This is something you must learn for yourself. No one can tell you. When the time comes, you will know."

Now Red Horse was *completely* confused.

13
>> >> >>

It was later the same day that they encountered the voyageurs. To Red Horse it was a complete surprise. They were moving well, having encountered a long stretch of good water. The canoes slipped silently along with scarcely a ripple.

Red Horse, seated just in front of Paint in the lead canoe, was daydreaming. His eyes were half closed, and the cool water slid rapidly past him on both sides. He could imagine what it might feel like to be a fish, darting effortlessly, slicing through the water like an arrow through the air. An arrow . . . or a bird. What would it feel like to fly, like the swallows nesting in the cut-banks along the stream? They could dart like an arrow, or like the silvery minnows that fled before the canoe's progress from time to time. Or like a hawk, maybe. Yes, that would be exciting . . . to dive like the falcon, wings half closed, plummeting toward her quarry at tremendous speed before the strike. Horse could imagine the tension, but also the thrill. It would be like riding a rapidly galloping horse across the prairie, the wind rushing past his ears . . . no, it would be smoother. There would be no bounce at all, as there would on the back of even the smoothest horse. It would be practically soundless, only the rush of the wind.

He wondered if a fish experienced the sound of water rushing past. It had no ears, as far as he knew, but it must hear, or *feel* noises. He would ask his father about that, sometime. Meanwhile, he watched the water slide past, and the slower movement of the irregular green wall of the willows on either side.

His reverie was interrupted by a low hiss from the negro behind him.

"Sst! Horse! Look ahead!"

The young man came fumbling up out of his daydream to see the nose of another canoe sliding into sight, perhaps a bow shot ahead. This was a completely unexpected sight, and Horse was wide awake in an instant. There was a murmur of talk in the canoe, and Blue Jacket, in the front, held up a hand for silence.

There were six men in the craft being paddled upstream by the newcomers. Red Horse recognized them quickly, though he did not know their names. He had seen them around the fort. Voyageurs, they were called. He did not exactly understand their status. They were French, but not soldiers. Perhaps they belonged to a different

warrior society . . . yes, that must be it. They
were tolerated, respected, even, but not completely trusted. He had noticed an irritation on
the part of Blue Jacket at times when dealing with
these men. Now he wondered how Blue Jacket
would react to this unexpected encounter. It was
quickly obvious that the canoe of the voyageurs
must have been following the trading party, only
a day or two behind. This, too, was curious.

The craft approached each other, circling
slightly as the expert canoemen sought a calmer
backwater near the shore, for a few moments of
conversation. Red Horse saw that the man in the
front of the strangers' canoe was one he had often
noticed at the fort. He was a large, powerful man,
with a heavy black beard. That alone was enough
to attract the attention of young Red Horse. He
was accustomed to the clean-plucked faces of the
People. The other thing about this man was his
obvious air of leadership. The man was a chief. A
sub-chief of some sort, no doubt. There was obviously a different pattern of leadership among
these French. But unmistakably, the man was a
leader. The attitude of the men around him had
always marked him as their spokesman.

"What are they doing here?" Red Horse whispered to Paint.

"Ssh . . . be still and listen."

The conversation was in French, of course. Red
Horse could follow some of it, but he was puzzled

by it. On the surface, it seemed to be only a calm discussion such as one might have with a friend.

"Hello, my friend," began Black Beard, with a wave of the hand and a broad smile that showed even white teeth, startling against the dark fur on his face. "A good morning."

"You are turning back?"

"Yes. The river is smaller upstream. Soon there will be no water."

"We had begun to see that. Well, so be it!"

"You will turn back too?" asked Blue Jacket.

Black Beard shrugged.

"Of course. If there is no water, one cannot paddle a boat." He smiled broadly again.

Red Horse was puzzled. On the surface, this was a pleasant and helpful conversation between friends. Why, then, did he have the feeling that there was more? It was a definite feeling, a tension in the air, a tightness in the entire attitude of everyone in the canoes. It was expressed, perhaps, in the loud, overly friendly tones of the black-bearded voyageur, and in the slightly higher pitch of the voice of Blue Jacket.

Perhaps Red Horse would not have caught this tension at all if he had known the words better. But, insecure about his understanding of the French, the young man had been tuned to the *tone* of the conversation. And that was a tone with undercurrents of emotion, of dislike and distrust. It was very much like the polite sign-talk between enemies, Red Horse thought. Yes, that was it.

In traveling the prairie, the nomadic hunters often encountered other tribes also on the move, to new seasonal camp sites. With their women and children present, it was too dangerous to engage in combat. Through the eons of time, a customary procedure had developed. There would be no fighting when the families were present. The opposing chiefs met, conversed about the weather and the hunt, and where they intended to camp. That was helpful to both, to avoid overhunting an area. Their seasonal camp sites could be easily located anyway. To an outside observer such a conversation, using hand-signs, might appear to be a casual contact between old friends.

And this was the way in which Red Horse saw the meeting in the canoes. It was a surprise to him, one he did not understand. But there was definitely the same air, the same feeling of tension and distrust. Why, when the two Frenchmen, Blue Jacket and Black Beard, were not only of the same tribe, but of the same village? *Aiee*, the ways of outsiders were indeed strange. This conversation was one which would have been appropriate for a chance meeting of enemies, who were not yet ready to fight.

The canoes circled, and that of Blue Jacket took the lead. His second canoe fell in behind, and that of Black Beard turned to follow in the rear, heading back downstream.

As their normal traveling pace resumed, Red Horse had another thought. Nowhere in the conversation had the secondary goal of Santa Fe been mentioned. That, of course, had been kept from the entire expedition until recently. It seemed that now it was to be kept secret from the voyageurs, even yet. He wondered if the soldiers would be cautioned not to mention it, or if they would simply know. Or maybe it did not even matter. He would ask Paint, but now did not seem a good time to do so.

It was not until they stopped for the night that opportunity arose.

"Paint," he asked the negro when they were alone, "do these voyageurs know about Santa Fe?"

The black man's eyes grew wide and round. Red Horse was beginning to recognize that expression. It was used when Paint thought that these were things that should not be spoken. It was a look of surprise, shock, and a little of fear. Of mock fear, at least. Red Horse was of the opinion that there was very little that Paint really feared. He was merely prudent.

"That," stated Paint positively, "is not for us to speak of."

He turned away, giving the definite impression that the conversation was over. At least on that subject.

"But Paint," Red Horse persisted, on a slightly

different trail, "I do not understand. Are these men enemies?"

"Enemies? No, of course not!"

"Then why are they not trusted?"

The black man did not answer for a little while. He picked up another buffalo chip and added it to the stack in the crook of his left arm.

"Horse," he said finally, "there are many things that I do not know. One of them is why leaders behave the way they do. Some of these things I do not *want* to know. For a slave . . . a prisoner, you said, it is bad to know too much."

Red Horse was astonished.

"But Paint!" he exclaimed, "Can it ever be bad to *learn?*"

The black man stared at him, and his face softened in understanding.

"Maybe not," Paint said whimsically. "Maybe not. But, it can be harmful to admit that you know. For me, it is safer to know very little. For you . . . I do not know . . . But anyone learns more if he says less. So, listen and learn."

Red Horse was frustrated. He was certain that Paint saw the apparent enmity between the two French chiefs. It must be that Paint's status as a prisoner made him at risk over this, whatever it was. He supposed that he could understand that. In a clash of power and prestige between two chiefs, it would be likely that prisoners would find themselves in a precarious position. Ah, well, he would watch and listen.

14
>> >> >>

LeFever was furious. He had half suspected that the voyageur, DuBois, might follow the expedition. There was no way to tell, of course. It was merely that DuBois was an opportunist. He was always on the lookout for any possibility that might arise that would allow him to attempt self-benefit. In the delicate balance of diplomacy between the trader, the natives, and the soldiers, DuBois was a factor over which the captain had no control whatever.

Even though he might dislike the trader, there had never been any proof that the man was dishonest. As for the natives, LeFever had no qualms at all. He tried to be forthright and fair with them, and had found that they reciprocated. The Kenzas had been most helpful in the establishment of the post.

But DuBois . . . it seemed that the man could easily upset the entire project. One incident . . . an unfair treatment of some Kenza, perhaps, might bring down the ill will of the whole Kenza nation. The natives would not distinguish the subtle differences between soldiers, traders, and voyageurs. They were all *French*, and would all reap the bitter fruit of DuBois's chicanery.

This reminded him of some French officers he had known, who failed to distinguish between various tribes of natives. After a problem with one group, or even one individual, they would immediately expand their resentment to include all natives, of all tribes. It made no sense, of course. It was as if some native, cheated by an Englishman, would assume that all whites were dishonest. Not only all English, but French too. Yes, all Europeans, even. Spanish, too. It was ridiculous, this attitude, but it was there, a smouldering coal, ready to break into flame when fanned by the winds of chance.

That, of course, was the importance of understanding on the frontier. Any slight incident could set in motion the enmity of large groups of natives.

So far, the French had been rather successful at the delicate game of diplomacy. Better, LeFever felt smugly, than the English, and the Spanish to the southwest. Ah, that war with the natives, a couple of decades ago . . . a bad thing! They had heard that the Spanish had now returned from Mexico, on apparently better terms. He hoped so. The establishment of trade with Santa Fe depended on it.

Honesty, that was the key, he believed. Treat others fairly, show that one is dependable and predictable, and others will be predictable also. This, then, was the source of his concern. He had no control over the honesty of others. There was no way that he could predict the actions of Baptiste DuBois. If there was anything predictable at all about the man, LeFever felt, it was his shady character. DuBois could be counted on for chicanery. It was doubly frustrating, then, that the voyageur could demand from the military the protection of the Crown. And LeFever was obligated to furnish it.

It was infuriating to know that the voyageurs had followed a sensitive expedition of this sort. It had taken all of his self-control to sit and make small talk with the grinning scoundrel in the other canoe. And now, on the return trip downriver, they were traveling together. The absolute *gall* of the man made LeFever grit his teeth until his jaw ached.

And now, another danger came to mind. He had announced to the soldiers the secondary purpose of the expedition, the search for the route to Santa Fe. They would be in contact, now, with the voyageurs, who would visit around the campfires at night, and there was no way to maintain secrecy. After all the carefully laid plans to map the route for trade with Spain, it would now be out in the open. The possibility of secrecy was gone forever. It could even develop into a race to establish diplomatic relations with the Spanish authorities before the voyageurs could reach Santa Fe.

He could, of course, forbid DuBois to make such contact. It involved another nation, and not merely native tribes. As military commandant of Fort de Chastaigne, he had the authority to issue such an edict. The problem was that of enforcement. There was nothing to prevent the voyageurs from moving at will, out onto the plains. LeFever was almost certain that it had happened before, probably repeatedly. Exploring parties, motivated by greed, could move without the sanction of the Crown, and undoubtedly had done so.

He hesitated to question DuBois. The man would deny any ulterior motives, of course. There would then be nothing else that LeFever could do. For a time he considered the possibility of such a confrontation, just to let the voyageurs know that he was aware of their movements. There might be some value in that. Unfortunately, there were two sides to that coin. If he revealed his knowledge of their activities, he also revealed his weakness. It would be plain that he could do nothing about it, and he would lose face. That, in turn, would make the voyageurs bolder, and his own authority weaker.

No, he decided, he must wait. He did not know what might be coming, but to act prematurely would be worse than doing nothing at all.

It was nearing evening. The three canoes were

making good time, moving with the current instead of against it, as on the outbound leg of the journey. They had only been obliged to portage once today. They should reach the Mandan town well before dark, and that would be a good place to stop for the night.

LeFever had announced such intentions earlier in the afternoon. This was met with enthusiastic agreement, especially from the voyageurs. Even this ready approval irritated him, because he recognized its insincerity. The attitude of DuBois was almost condescending.

They rounded a curve of the river's course. A startled blue heron, interrupted at its fishing, beat its way into the air. It was clumsy and ungainly for the first few strokes, but quickly gained equilibrium and became a creature of grace and beauty as it rose above the trees. LeFever envied the bird its freedom to rise above the trees and leave behind any possible threat to its safety.

He was still watching the bird when there was an exclamation behind him. The others in the canoe were pointing ahead. A thin haze of smoke hung lazily in an ill-defined layer over the river and the trees ahead.

"The village!" someone said, and they moved on downstream.

If LeFever had been concerned before, this contact with the Mandans did nothing to relieve his anxiety. It was not the welcome that they received. That was a gratifying thing, like a happy reunion. Yet, he could not fail to notice that the greatest honor and attention was not directed primarily at himself, but at Baptiste DuBois and his party of voyageurs.

DuBois, of course, had spent some time in this village, probably overnight, since the captain and his party passed through. They would have given lavish gifts and attempted to establish a better relationship than that of the soldiers. It would not be difficult, given the second chance at contact.

LaFontaine, the trader, sat grimly watching the merriment. LeFever had not talked with him about his concerns. He had not entirely trusted the trader. There was a time, he recalled, when he had actually suspected that there might be some sort of conspiracy involving the trader and the voyageurs. Now, watching the resentment on the face of LaFontaine, he realized that that had been a wrong impression. The trader was not the threat here.

He had misjudged that situation, he told himself. Perhaps he resented the trader's political leverage, which had achieved the trading franchise. One never knew the background of such things. The trading privilege was bestowed by the governor of the region, whose office, in turn, was political. The trader might be a relative of the governor, or one he owed a favor. Such a political plum as this exclusive trading franchise might even be purchased. Sometimes it was obvious, the reason for the appointment. Most often, not. In

the case of LaFontaine, no one was really certain.
It was assumed that some gold may have changed
hands.

No matter . . . the trader was here, at least for
the present. LeFever must accept him as an ally.
The manner in which the entire situation was
moving made this seem necessary. DuBois was attempting to undermine the authority of the military, even while relying on their protection.
LeFever wished that he had a bit more respect for
the trader, if he was to be allied with him against
the threat of the voyageur. Yet it was difficult to
accept the fact that the man allowed his wife to
behave as she did. Ah, he now realized, that must
be the basis for his dislike. A man not forceful
enough to keep his wife from flirting with every
man at the post. That, her husband should not
allow.

The captain got no farther than that in his
thinking. Not being a husband yet himself, he
was not certain what he would do about it in the
trader's place. Try to keep the woman so appeased
that she would not have to think of other men,
he supposed. That possibility certainly had an ap-
peal to it. But, in the final analysis, he had no way
to know. Maybe he had misjudged the trader.
Maybe he, too, was trapped in a situation over
which he had little control. Possibly even life itself was like that, and no one ever controls his
destiny.

He resolved to be more charitable toward the

trader. Tonight, even, he would seek out the man to talk with him, to outline some future plans. Yes, he had been remiss, he realized, in his preoccupation with the building of the fort. He had not worked closely enough with LaFontaine, a potential ally.

He rose from where he had been eating, and sauntered toward the little fire where the trader sat, with a couple of his employees. A native approached him, signing a greeting and gestures of respect. LeFever returned the hand-signs, pleased that he was able to do so. He was not prepared for the next thing that happened. The man made the hand-sign for "give" and pointed to himself. *"Give me,"* thought LeFever. *What . . . ?*

The next sign was plainly that for "drink." Odd, with the river only a few steps away. He started to point there and sign for "water," but stopped short. The native, a well-built man of middle age, was swaying slightly, and there was a silly grin on his face. Just then, a shift in the breeze brought an unmistakable hint of brandy. *Sacrebleu,* the man was drunk!

Rage swept over him. He was barely able to sign something approximating "I have no drink," and pushed on past. *Damn* that DuBois, giving brandy to these people. The drunken native stood there, still swaying but no longer grinning. He tossed an obscene gesture after the retreating figure.

LeFever did not see the voyageur, but strode on, searching for him. This was too much, and could endanger them all. He had suspected that DuBois had sold brandy to his troops, but had no proof. But this . . .

It was probably a good thing that, at the height of his anger, he could not find DuBois. One of the other voyageurs shrugged.

"I do not know, monsieur," he answered the inquiry. "Maybe he looks for a woman."

The voyageur giggled and gave a conspiratorial leer, which further angered the captain. He wheeled and strode off, more angry and frustrated than he had ever been.

15

>> >> >>

White Fox had quickly sensed the power struggle between the two French chiefs. It was a situation that could become dangerous. He had experienced enough danger from contact with other cultures to make him wary, and quite alert to such things.

He had been pleased with the reaction of his son to this entire expedition. Red Horse was learning many things. It was good to see the boy learning the language of the soldiers, and asking questions of the black man, Paint. That was a strange thing, completely outside the experience of White Fox. Not that it was unusual to have a prisoner. All tribes took prisoners occasionally. Usually, though, such captive status did not last long. A prisoner might be released, or killed, or even adopted into the tribe, but it would happen fairly quickly. The idea that people with dark skins could remain prisoners forever . . . yes, even the next generation and the next . . . *aiee,* that was strange! At first, Fox had had a problem deciding whether the black man had been painted that way to mark his status. At Fort de Chastaigne, it was apparent that only those with black skins were the permanent prisoners. But were they slaves because of the dark skin, or had they been painted because they were slaves?

Red Horse had talked much of this, and had asked many questions of Paint. It was now known that Paint's people were born that way, and were already prisoners from before their birth. A strange thing! But it was good for Red Horse to see such strange customs.

But the other, the conflict between the French themselves . . . that appeared more dangerous. Any power struggle could be unsettling to the bystanders. Fox had seen it in his own tribe. One of the bands would have a bad season, and their chief would lose prestige. There were always subchiefs ready to take advantage of the shifting weight of prestige. Usually things would settle down, sometimes with the loss of a few families who preferred to join another band rather than participate in the squabble.

There had been an argument, Fox recalled, a generation ago, which split the Eastern band. Two families and their children had left the band. Instead of joining one of the other bands, however, they had camped by themselves, and had been killed by the Forest People. Well, their poor judgement had been the cause. The Eastern band had always been noted for foolish ways. Ultimately, the only survivor of that episode was South Wind, now his wife and mother of their son, Red Horse.

The tension that White Fox saw growing among the French could lead to great problems, he feared. Increasingly, he had the feeling that none of the three chiefs really liked each other. And of course, one who is disliked is usually distrusted. Of the three, Blue Jacket appeared to have the most actual authority. The trader worked with him, or was apparently supposed to do so. The trader was a difficult man to understand, however. No real leadership qualities were apparent, and White Fox wondered how he had become a chief . . . even a sub-chief. His followers, it seemed, were *paid* to follow him, and in addition he had several of the black-skinned slaves. But none of his people really seemed to feel the allegiance they should. Even the soldiers of Blue Jacket, who were understood to be there for pay, had more loyalty to their chief.

Both of these chiefs seemed to resent the presence of the Black Beard chief. He was another question in the mind of Fox. His followers seemed quite loyal . . . maybe Blue Jacket and the trader resented that, since their people did not . . . ah, well, the ways of the French were strange. Probably there was no way he could ever understand it.

He did notice increasing tension after they

reached the Mandan village, however. It seemed to be centered around the way the Black Beard chief and his party dealt with the Mandans. They were interested in the women of the village. It was understandable. They had no women of their own, and had been on the river for some time. It was also true of the soldiers and the trader's men. In such circumstances he might have been interested himself. He saw no harm in it, and many of the Mandans welcomed the chance for temporary alliances.

It would not have been so among the People, whose marriage customs were stricter, but to each his own customs. So, he saw the men of the exploring party offering small gifts to the men of the village in return for the favors of their wives or daughters. Some readily agreed.

One of the voyageurs stood and bartered with a villager using sign-talk. It seemed that the Frenchman was offering some beads and a mirror, and the Mandan kept refusing, making the sign for drink. Finally White Fox understood, when the voyageur drew out a flask of liquid and offered it. The other man nodded eagerly, and the two walked off together toward one of the lodges.

A little later, White Fox encountered Blue Jacket, who seemed quite upset and angry. Fox avoided any direct contact, but by quiet observation gathered that there was a problem over the gifts. The voyageurs were a bit more lavish with gifts than the soldiers. As a result, the people of the host village were ignoring Blue Jacket and his soldiers, and treating Black Beard and his men with great respect.

A little later, White Fox saw a man reeling dizzily across the clearing. At first Fox thought he was sick, but then he saw that the man carried a bottle of the dark fluid that the French regarded so highly. Fox had tasted it once himself, at the fort. It was warm and sweet as it touched his tongue, but quickly began to burn. *Instead of going down, it goes up,* he had thought, trying to maintain his composure and refrain from sneezing. He did not like the stuff, though in a little while he felt warm and good, and wise. That was odd, because when he awoke sometime later, his head ached and he did not feel wise at all.

The brandy affected different people differently, he had noticed. Some men became angry and wanted to fight, some became sad. And now, from what he could tell, a great part of Blue Jacket's anger was because the voyageurs were giving brandy to the Mandans. *Why should he care?* White Fox wondered to himself. Was there something about the way this hot-tasting fluid altered the spirit that worried Blue Jacket? Or was it only that the soldier chief was angry at his own loss of prestige?

It would be some time until dark, but already there was much shouting and singing and ribald merriment. Somewhere outside the village a woman squealed and laughed. Nearer at hand, two men argued over a young woman while she awaited the outcome. Apparently it did not matter to her, and she finally left with both men. A Mandan sat, leaning against the wall of a lodge, semi-stuporous, with a bottle in his lap.

White Fox was concerned. Even with his people's traditional tolerance for the customs of others, no matter how strange, this . . . *aiee!* He was not certain why he felt this uneasiness. Maybe the frightening change in the spirit of the village that he saw before his eyes.

He went to rejoin his wife at their campfire, near that of Blue Jacket. Two of the voyageurs were standing there, offering South Wind a handful of beads. Fox could see the anger in her face, and he felt his own temper rising.

"Go away!" he snapped, using hand-signs as well as French. "This is my woman!"

One of the men turned away, but the other seemed inclined to argue. White Fox was rapidly becoming angrier.

"What is this?" demanded an authoritative French voice behind him.

He turned to see the furious Blue Jacket, practically trembling with rage. The tirade was so rapid that Fox, with his meager understanding of French, could not follow it. There was no doubt, however, that the captain was outraged. The voyageur turned, with an almost insolent sneer, and stalked away. Blue Jacket turned back to face South Wind.

"My apologies, madam," he said formally.

South Wind did not know the words, but the meaning and intent was clear.

"It is nothing," she signed.

"You are not hurt?"

"No, no," she laughed.

The captain nodded and turned away, and they could see the frustration in every move of his body.

"I am sorry," began White Fox, "I should have stayed with you."

South Wind smiled.

"I could have handled it myself," she said calmly, not moving from where she sat.

Gently, she lifted the edge of her buckskin dress. There on the ground beside her lower leg lay her flint knife. Fox smiled in recognition. She had nearly killed him with that very knife the first time they met, believing him to be an enemy. *Yes*, he thought, *she could take care of herself.*

"But you should not have to," he said aloud. "I will stay closer to our fire."

Another thought came to him.

"Where is Red Horse?" he asked.

"I do not know," Wind answered. "Is there danger?"

He paused a moment before he answered.

"I do not know," he admitted, "but Wind, I do not like the spirit of this place."

"It has a bad spirit?" she asked, puzzled.

"I . . . no, that is not it . . . there are things

happening that I do not understand. The spirit of these things is bad, maybe. Not the *place.*"

To himself, he wondered if he should go and look for Red Horse.

"Is our son with the black man?" he asked.

"I think not, Fox," South Wind answered. "He was, earlier."

White Fox decided not to go searching. For one thing, he did not want to leave Wind alone. *Aiee,* why had they come on this journey, anyway? He wished they were at home in the Tallgrass prairie, with the Southern band.

16
>> >> >>

Red Horse watched the progress of the evening with detached interest. A more important objective was on his mind. He was on constant watch for the girl who had so impressed him before. The Girl-Who-Smiled, and who looked much like Swallow, back home among the People.

They had been in the village for some time before he encountered her. She gave him the glorious smile that he remembered. It was like the brightness of the sun after a storm, and the heart of Red Horse was very good.

"I have looked for you," he said in hand-signs.

The girl laughed, a clear rippling sound that thrilled him through and through.

"It is good," she signed.

"How are you called?" Red Horse asked.

"I am Rabbit Woman," the girl signed back.

She laughed as if there were a joke, but he did not notice.

"How are you called?" she asked in turn.

"I am Red Horse."

She nodded.

"It is a strong name," she signed.

He did not know how to proceed next, or what he actually wanted. He considered several approaches, and rejected each as either too forward or too childish. Finally Rabbit Woman, seeming to sense his predicament, signed again.

"Look! Would you wish to meet me later?"

"Yes, yes!" he signed.

She laughed, and he was embarrassed to have appeared so eager.

"It is good! Just before dark . . . upstream, there is a clearing with a dead cottonwood tree on the ground . . . I will be there."

She flashed the sunny smile again, and touched his arm briefly. Then she turned and was gone.

Aiee! Red Horse was numb with happiness, and as dizzy and confused as some of the men he saw consuming the fiery brandy-drink. He stumbled absentmindedly along, unable to concentrate on anything else. Repeatedly he checked the position of the sun. Sun Boy seemed to stand still today, instead of proceeding on his daily torch-run. *Aiee*, the day was slow.

It was far from dusk when Red Horse could stand it no longer. Shadows were barely beginning to lengthen as he made his way upstream. He would find the clearing, would be there before Rabbit Woman. That would be good . . . it would show the sincerity of his interest.

Pleased with himself, he followed a dim path along the river, as she had indicated. Ahead, there seemed to be a clearing, and his steps quickened. He wondered how long he would have to wait before the girl arrived. He brushed aside the last dogwood branch and started to step into the open. There, across the clearing, lay the trunk of a massive cottonwood, weathered now to silvery gray. Yes, this must be the place.

A hint of movement caught his eye, and he shifted his gaze to look. Two figures, locked in romantic embrace, rolled on the soft grass of the clearing. One was a voyageur, and the other a shapely woman. As their position shifted a little, he could see the woman's face. Their eyes met, and her face brightened in recognition. To his astonishment, he saw the smile, the Girl-Who-Smiled. He stood a moment, frozen in disbelief. His spirit was crushed, betrayed. There was no mistaking it, the same sunny, cheerful and inviting smile that had thrilled him earlier. But now it was different. The smile that he had assumed was for him alone now shone for him over the shoulder of the man in her arms. The whole thing was obscene! How could she lie there and smile, friendly and unconcerned, while even as their eyes met she was . . . *aiee*, it was too much. He turned away, the image of that smiling, beautiful face, those twinkling eyes, now a mockery. How could she . . . ?

The voyageur, totally preoccupied, had not

even seen the intruder. Red Horse would soon leave. If he had not arrived early for the tryst, he would never have known, and Rabbit Woman would have welcomed him with the same enthusiasm he had just seen. *How stupid,* he thought. How naive and inexperienced he had been. Rabbit Woman. *Aiee,* that was the joke! Red Horse's heart was very heavy.

He must get away. He fled, back down the path, choking back tears of disappointment and embarrassment. But he could not go back to the village just now, he realized. He must be alone, a little while, to regain his composure. He turned away from the river, and started toward a rocky hillock a hundred paces south of the stream. There he found a secluded niche among the jumbled stones, and sat down, nursing his grief.

It was much later that he saw two figures approaching from the direction of the village. It had been fully dark for some time, and the moon was just rising. Red Horse did not feel much better, but was trying to accept the disappointment. He was at least able to think of other things. The night sounds . . . a coyote in the distance, the call of a night bird, the raucous cry of a green heron downriver.

But now . . . the two were unaware of his presence. A man and a woman, probably looking for a spot for romance. Recent memory tugged at his heart. Should he make his presence known?

He was about to rise and leave when he sensed that something was not right. He had assumed that the two shadowy forms were closely blended because their arms were embracing each other. But no . . . the man, a large and powerful man, seemed to be dragging the young woman along, half carrying her, while she struggled weakly.

They came close, and the man paused, looking around for a spot . . . the girl struggled and he cuffed her across the side of the head, and threw her to the ground. Red Horse saw in the moonlight that her hands were tied. He assumed that a gag had also been placed in her mouth to keep her from screaming. He did not know what to do. This was certainly not right. The girl was clearly unwilling. But her tormenter was big . . . now he recognized the black-bearded leader of the voyageurs.

Red Horse was physically afraid. There was no way he could help the girl, and no way he could leave, even, without being seen. Then, out of the darkness came another man, one of the Mandans, who began to shout at Black Beard. He was a young man, little older than Red Horse.

The situation was now apparent. This was the husband or sweetheart of the girl on the ground, who had been abducted by Black Beard. Ah, thought Red Horse, not all Mandans are as free with the use of their women as some. This one was enraged. Without even pausing in his tirade, he bent to cut the thongs on the girl's wrists.

Red Horse barely saw the kick coming, and the Mandan husband not at all. The voyageur's boot struck upward at the unprotected face, knocking the man half senseless. In an instant Black Beard had dropped upon the man, plunging a knee into his stomach as he drove a knife into the chest.

The girl had scrambled to her feet, pulling the scraps of thongs from her wrists, and the gag from her mouth. She screamed then, and fled toward the village, still screaming and yelling. Black Beard sprinted after her, but it was apparent that his pursuit was futile. The girl would reach help before the big man could catch her.

Red Horse rose and hurried to the side of the wounded man. The Mandan, who seemed still only half conscious, was moaning softly. The wound, in the side of the chest, may have been partially deflected, it seemed. It did not appear fatal. Well, Red Horse reasoned, he could do nothing here. The girl would bring help. He felt a certain danger to himself, as he had witnessed the attack. He rose and started for the village.

Ahead of him he could hear yelling and angry voices. He trotted upstream a way, to come in from a different direction. He approached the campfire of his parents to find them sleepily rising from their sleeping robes.

"What is it?" asked South Wind. "Are you all right?"

"Of course, Mother."

"What has happened?"

"I do not know," he lied.

Maybe he would tell his father later what he had heard and seen. For now, he was afraid for his own safety. He was concerned, of course, for the wounded man on the hill. But he was more afraid of what Black Beard would do if he learned that Red Horse had seen the entire event.

17
>> >> >>

LeFever lay staring at the sky, unable to sleep. There are many things that may interfere with sleep, and he was finding that one major factor here was anger. He was being forced to assert himself, and was not able to decide how to do it. With his soldiers, he had no trouble maintaining the strict discipline of the military. In his relations with LaFontaine, the trader, he could work it out. They *must* work together, and both knew it.

But the voyageur, DuBois . . . the man had gone too far. It was bad enough to curry favor with the tribes as DuBois had done. But to brazenly trade brandy . . . yes, he had even supplied the liquor to the soldiers too, judging from the condition of some of them. There would be a reckoning on *that* score, at least. That, he could enforce.

About what to do with DuBois, he was still at a loss. He could ban all trading with the natives, except by LaFontaine, but he knew it could not be

enforced. DuBois was a civilian, and could come
and go as he pleased. Once out of sight, there was
no way to prevent any act that the scoundrel
might devise, and then deny all knowledge of. For
the hundredth time LeFever came back to the
same realization. He was completely without authority where civilians were concerned. His com-
mission stated that in the region administered by
Fort de Chastaigne, including all territory to the
west, he carried the authority of the Crown. But
the Crown was far away. He supposed that, in
principle, he could order DuBois arrested, even
executed. Yet he had no real evidence of a crime
worthy of capital punishment. And, when one
dealt with civilians, it could ruin even a bright
future in the military. Many young officers had
found that, to their sorrow.

He must confront DuBois, of course. The prospect, and the predictable reaction, angered him
even further. DuBois would be overly polite, condescending, even fawning over the reprimand.
The man would assume an air of injured innocence, denying any intention whatever to cause
any problems. All the while he would be laughing
to himself behind that damned beard, amused at
the helplessness of the military.

LeFever rolled to his other side, still seeking
sleep. There was no position that seemed comfortable. He knew it was in his mind, this torment,
but it translated to physical discomfort.

The sounds of revelry were quieting some, finally. It must be past the midnight hour, he thought, and it was high time. He had not interfered, knowing that he could not be everywhere at once. He could, however, inflict the strictest of discipline on his troops, and would certainly do so tomorrow. It would be a long time before any of these men would be guilty of such breach of discipline again.

He was just planning how he would phrase his scathing speech of reprimand, when the scream came. It was from some distance away from the river. A woman's scream, in pain or terror. There was a brief pause, and the screaming subsided, to be replaced by a young woman's voice shouting an alarm of some sort. He did not have enough understanding of the Mandan tongue to get the full meaning of her words, but it was obviously an alarm.

His first thought was that the woman had been attacked by a wild animal, perhaps a bear or a wolf. Then he realized that such an interpretation was only wishful thinking. A young woman would not have ventured that far from the village alone. Someone else was with her, probably a man . . . one of the voyageurs, or even one of his soldiers. LeFever's anger rose at the thought. No matter what the problem was, it was likely that one of the French party was involved, and possibly to blame for the outcry.

He was rolling from his bed, trying to look in the direction of the commotion. There was a movement on the slope, a suggestion of someone, maybe two persons, running toward the village in the moonlight. People were rousing, the natives bobbing out of their thatched houses, the French rolling sleepily out of their blankets.

"Sergeant!" LeFever yelled, "Have the men look alive!"

At least his unit would not be caught off guard in case of trouble.

Fires were flaring up, pushing back the darkness, as people tossed sticks on embers, creating flames for light. A young woman ran into the village, still yelling, and a crowd gathered around her. Then, out of the dark strode DuBois, arrogant and confident. The girl pointed accusingly, still shouting. *Damn!* thought LeFever, *What has he done?* Several of the native men left the group, to run back up the slope toward the original point of the girl's scream. There was an angry mutter from the Mandans.

DuBois looked around, and caught the captain's eye. The man actually *smiled.*

"What could I do, Captain? The bastard tried to knife me!"

That would have solved many problems, thought LeFever. Aloud, he spoke sharply.

"What *were* you doing?"

"Just a little romance, Captain. No harm. You can understand, no?"

There was a leer on the voyageur's face now.

"You bastard," LeFever gritted between

clenched teeth. "You may have gotten us all killed."

"No, no," DuBois said soothingly. "Any of these savages will rent a woman for a few trinkets or some brandy. No harm."

LeFever struggled to stay calm.

"DuBois," he snapped, his voice high and tight, "you have found one who would not. What did you do?"

"Gave him a taste of steel, m'sieur."

He touched his knife hilt suggestively.

"You *killed* the man?"

DuBois shrugged.

"Who knows?"

How in God's name has this man lived this long? LeFever wondered. *Someone should have cleansed the world of him already.*

"Sergeant," LeFever called softly. "Pass the word . . . be ready to board the canoes. Leave the packs if we must. No one is to fire without an order."

"Yes, Captain," the sergeant called back.

Now the men who had run up the slope were returning, carrying a limp form. LeFever shouldered forward.

"Is he alive?" he asked in hand-signs.

He was greeted with bitter, angry stares.

"Yes," one of the rescue party finally acknowledged.

LeFever elected a dignified retreat, and withdrew carefully from the point of action. He would like to take his party and leave, but did not wish to appear frightened. Besides, it would be a diplomatic thing to apologize. He made his way through the crowd, seeking one of the chiefs. He saw many glances of hate. It was as he feared. These people would make no distinction between one Frenchman and another.

He finally saw the man he sought, and altered his course in that direction. He was met with a cold stare.

"Greetings, my brother! My heart is sad because of the trouble," he signed.

The chief's stern expression did not change.

"We have welcomed you as friends," he answered, also in hand-signs, "and this is how you thank us. Your hearts are not good."

"Some of our young men are foolish," LeFever persisted. "They do foolish things."

"This is greater than foolish. Gray Fox may be dying. It is best you leave!"

"It is good, my chief. We will do so now."

He turned and barked orders to the sergeant. Word passed quickly, and the nervous outsiders began to withdraw toward the canoes. An old woman hobbled forward and spat at LeFever. The spittle trickled down his blue jacket, and he tried to ignore it.

White Fox, having had experience in such confrontations, was moving his wife toward the river, closely followed by their son. The voyageurs, camped a stone's throw downstream, were busily loading their canoes, hurrying the laggards along with much yelling and exhortation. By contrast, LeFever was proud of the quiet way his soldiers moved, swift and efficient.

The first canoe of the soldiers was now ready. The captain gave the command and the soldiers pushed away, turned the craft to point downstream, and slipped into the night. His second canoe was also loaded, and after accounting for everyone, he stepped in. As his soldiers prepared to shove off, he turned to look at DuBois. The voyageur was brazenly making his way toward his waiting canoe, pelted with sticks, stones, and debris. Such missiles were also striking the canoe of LeFever, or splattering into the water. He ordered the soldiers to push away from shore.

Thus far, they had been pelted only with insults and trash. No weapons had been used. Now, however, LeFever saw a man dash forward, carrying a short ax. It came to him that this might be the father of the girl, or perhaps of her husband, the young man who lay near death. He tried to shout a warning as the angry warrior charged down on DuBois, but could not make himself heard above the din. At the last possible moment, the voyageur turned and saw his assailant. He snatched a pistol from his belt, pointed, and fired.

The roar of the explosion shattered the night, echoing across the river and back again from the distant hills. There was shocked silence from the crowd for a moment. The man with the upraised ax stood erect for an instant, then toppled backward. A young woman ran forward to kneel beside him.

DuBois calmly stuck his pistol back into his belt, and stepped into his waiting canoe. They pushed away from the shore just as the angry crowd surged forward. A few arrows arched toward the canoe as it turned and followed the others, slipping out of sight into the darkness.

18
>> >> >>

It seemed that the night would never end. There was only one direction to travel, and that was downstream. On long smooth stretches of deep water, the oarsmen paused and drifted, everyone silent and listening for sounds of pursuit. There was nothing to indicate such pursuit, only the night sounds. On the other hand, there was no reassurance, no proof that they were *not* followed. They dared not stop to see. To do so would, if they were being pursued, destroy all chance of escape.

So they pushed on, in the watery light of the half-moon, pausing at times to get out of the canoes and wade and drag them over a riffle. At dawn, LeFever called a halt on a gravel bar to assess their situation. His temper was short, and it was apparent that he would tolerate no questioning of his orders from anyone.

There were three injuries from the shower of arrows, sticks, and stones that had pelted them as they embarked. All were among the voyageurs, in the last canoe to leave shore. One was a serious wound, a bubbling hole in the upper chest where an arrow had struck. The man's companions had yanked the shaft out, but his condition was not good. Pink froth formed around the hole in response to his labored breathing, and his color was ashen.

White Fox signed his willingness to help, and after a brief pause the captain nodded consent. The medicine man took a gourd of ointment from his pack to anoint the wound, then covered the bubbling froth with a scrap of buckskin, which he bound tightly around the chest. This seemed to make the wounded man more comfortable. At least, his breathing seemed easier.

"He may be bleeding inside," White Fox indicated privately to the captain. "I cannot tell. He will be better or worse tomorrow."

The other wounds were less threatening. One man had been struck by an arrow through the fleshy part of the upper arm. They pushed the arrow on through, and the bleeding did not seem unduly heavy.

One man had suffered a long slash across the left shoulder and arm. In the scramble to reach the canoe, there had been much jostling and shoving, and it was not until later that he realized he was bleeding. Someone had used a knife.

In addition, a thrown rock had raised a plum-colored lump on the brow of one of the soldiers, partially closing his eye.

Captain LeFever spoke briefly before they resumed travel.

"We do not know whether we are followed," he admitted. "We cannot stop to see. So, we go on. Also, they can travel as fast as we can, so we do not stop to camp and sleep."

There was a mutter among the men, which subsided quickly. It was apparent that the captain was in no mood to have his authority doubted, even by the civilians.

"We must remember, too," he continued, "that they may send runners to the towns below. We may have to fight our way downstream. So keep your weapons at hand."

There were nods of agreement, and a few furtive glances at the thin strip of timber along the river.

"Now, let us move!"

The canoes were quickly launched. During the procedure, however, LeFever managed to speak to DuBois aside.

"I will deal with you later, no?"

The voyageur did not answer, but withdrew into a sullen mood that was in a way more threatening than open defiance. He stepped into the canoe, seemingly undaunted.

This was most frustrating to LeFever. At times he almost wished that the big voyageur *would* challenge him. There was certainly enough transgression now to justify any punishment he might select. He could have the scoundrel put in irons, except, of course, that he had no irons. He would arrest DuBois, he had decided, when they arrived at the fort. DuBois could be charged with interfering with trade and goodwill among the natives. Beyond that, LeFever had not decided.

The thing which angered him most was not the threat to the fur trade. This Mandan town was somewhat distant for such trade anyway. They could concentrate on trade with the Kenzas and nearby Mandans and Pawnees. In a year or two the incident might be forgotten, and they could push the fur trade westward again.

But this could be a real threat to their secondary purpose, the establishment of trade with the Spanish in Santa Fe. LeFever was not certain what White Fox had intended to convey about the route to the Spanish colonies. "Farther south," he had said. But *how far?* Possibly the route lay far enough to the south to be out of the sphere of Mandan influence. But again, possibly *not.* This might easily be a continuing danger, a barrier to the Spanish trade. *Damn the man!* His arrogance, his disregard . . . ah, well . . . It would be best not to think of it, LeFever realized. It would only cause him more worry and anger. He could deal with it later.

But again, DuBois had killed a man during their escape. At least it appeared so. Maybe the young husband who had tried to rescue his wife would survive the stabbing, but it was unlikely that the shooting victim would. The blow of a lead ball as large as a man's thumb, smashing into muscle and bone at point-blank range . . . well, he had seen how the man was slammed backward by the force of the impact.

That afternoon they passed another village on the north shore. The people waved cheerfully, remembering the party from their stop on the way upriver. This would seem to indicate that no runner had yet reached here with news of the killing. Of course, one might arrive at any time. It was too dangerous to consider stopping. They might also be pursued on the river. LeFever led the party past, near the opposite bank, allowing his men to wave back, but do or say nothing else. They moved on.

Red Horse was all but overwhelmed by the major happenings of the past day. He had been thrust into the depths of disappointment and despair by the actions of the girl . . . *aiee*, he still did not want to think of it. And that he could have believed she reminded him of Swallow . . . Swallow would never behave like that!

But overriding his hurt was the other . . . he had seen a man stabbed, for defending his wife. He had a difficult time accepting that Black Beard would do such a thing. But clearly the voyageur had intended to kill. He had actually done so, later. Red Horse's concern now was for his own safety. A man who would do such things would surely think nothing of killing a boy who had seen the treacherous attack.

He found himself watching Black Beard when opportunity offered, as they traveled. Once their eyes met, and a moment of panic gripped Red Horse. *He knows*, he thought to himself. *He saw me there in the rocks!* Black Beard turned away, and the panic eased, but the concern remained. He was not certain, but it seemed unlikely . . . well, he could avoid being alone with Black Beard.

He wished he could talk with someone. His father, perhaps, but there was no chance in the hurried pace of canoe travel. Or Paint . . . yes, the black man might know what to do.

It was not until next day that an opportunity offered. They had traveled all through the night, and everyone was exhausted and irritable. Red Horse's legs were beginning to ache from the constant cramped position in the canoe. From the way that the others sat or shifted uncomfortably, he knew that they, too, were experiencing the discomfort.

Just when he thought he could stand it no longer, Blue Jacket called a halt. A wide, sandy beach offered a stopping place.

"We will stop a little while," the captain called. "Walk to loosen the legs. Maybe we are not followed."

Gratefully, but somewhat stiffly, the men piled

out of the canoes, hobbling a few steps at first. Red Horse sought out the negro, and fell into step beside him.

"Paint, I want to talk to you."

"About the girl? You found her?"

The black man's eyes twinkled.

"I . . . well, yes, I *found* her, but . . . I did not . . . no, something else."

"Not the girl?"

"No, she was with another man."

Paint nodded in understanding.

"Too bad."

"No, Paint, something else. I saw Black Beard try to kill that man."

"The one who was stabbed?"

"Yes! I was there!"

"Ah! Was it as he said?"

"No. He kicked the man when he was not looking . . . the woman was tied and her mouth stuffed with something."

"She was *tied?*"

"Yes, Paint, he dragged her there."

The negro paused a moment, a concerned look on his face. He glanced around nervously.

"Keep walking," he said. "Horse, this is not good. DuBois, the Black Beard, is a bad one. You saw him shoot the man?"

"Yes."

"The natives will not take kindly to this . . . the woman, the stabbing, the killing . . . we must tell the captain."

He paused a moment, then spoke again.

"No, that is dangerous. You have told no one? Your parents?"

"No, no one."

"Good. Now this is what you should do. Tell no one at all. Only me. Black Beard does not know you saw?"

"I do not think so."

"He must not find out. He would try to stop you from telling." Paint drew a forefinger suggestively in a slashing motion across his throat. "We will tell the captain later, when we reach the fort. But stay away from Black Beard!"

Red Horse needed no urging. He doubted that he could sleep, knowing what he did, and knowing that Black Beard would try to stop him from telling it.

"What will Blue Jacket do?" he asked anxiously.

"When we reach the fort, he will make Black Beard a prisoner," Paint predicted. "For now, say nothing. But it is good that you have told me."

The sergeant was shouting now, calling the party back together to go on. The two hurried back toward the canoes.

As they approached, Red Horse saw two of the voyageurs on hands and knees, digging in the sand. The others stood and watched.

"What are they doing?" he asked his father.

"They are burying their dead," White Fox said soberly. "The one who was struck by the arrow."

He pointed at his own chest. "He died when they took him from the boat."

"They do not mourn him?" Horse asked.

"Not with songs, as we do. I do not know, my son."

"This is not a good burial, Father. The sand will shift with the next flood."

"Yes."

They turned away toward the canoes, while the voyageurs rolled the still, blanket-wrapped form into a shallow hole and began to scratch the sand over it.

19
>> >> >>

It was two more days before Captain LeFever allowed the pace to slacken. There had been no suggestion of pursuit, and the villages they passed showed no alarm. Their reception was warm and welcome. At one town they paused to rest, and the captain carried on a brief conversation with the chiefs, carefully monitored by White Fox.

At the instruction of LeFever, White Fox explained that there had been a misunderstanding. A few sleeps upstream a man had been accidently killed, and there was some ill feeling. The captain felt it more diplomatic to acknowledge a problem. It could not be concealed anyway. All the Mandan towns would know very quickly. Pawnees too, probably. At this point it was important not to abandon relations already established. So it was necessary to openly explain that there was a potential problem. LeFever was pleased that the chiefs nodded in understanding. Once again he was impressed that these tribes responded well if they were treated openly and fairly.

In retrospect, he now wished that he had stopped at the first Mandan towns on their retreat, to tell them of the encounter. But no, that would have been unwise. What if they had reacted with hostility? What if there had been pursuit by the people who had been wronged by DuBois? No, it would have been too risky. His mere handful of French would have been helpless before the hordes of angry Mandans who *could* have attacked them.

Now, in light of the friendly understanding they were encountering, he even considered going back upstream for a diplomatic contact or two. In the end, he decided against it. He had been able to plant the seeds of understanding. Soon word would filter down to the fort as to the feeling of the tribes. The Kenzas, with whom they had good communication, would have information very quickly. Yes, it would be better to move on, but at a more leisurely pace.

LeFever had already decided, however, not to camp at any of the villages they would pass. They would stop to talk, helping to reinforce their side of the regrettable incident upriver, but not remain overnight. He did not trust the voyageurs. It was conceivable, even, that DuBois might create yet another crisis if he were allowed contact with the natives.

LeFever had had a brief conversation with Du-

Bois during one of their rest stops. The voyageur was still sullen and noncommunicative. He spoke of regret, but very shortly and without much conviction. The captain saw little to indicate a repentant nature.

"You realize," the captain had said, "that it will be necessary to take formal action of some sort."

The voyageur nodded glumly, with no real answer.

"When we reach the fort, then," LeFever finished.

In truth, he had not yet decided what action he would take. As military commandant, his authority was almost unlimited. He could probably even hang the treacherous voyageur. But there would be the necessity to justify such an act with his superiors. Had a hanging offense actually been committed? Ultimately, the military governor of the district was the authority to whom he would answer. That, of course, was a political appointment, and he did not know the background. He must be cautious. The voyageur probably did not have friends in high places, but one never knew . . .

An easy solution might be to banish DuBois from this area, from Fort de Chastaigne's sphere of authority. That seemed tempting. If DuBois did have the political influence that LeFever feared, he could obtain a written letter of marque, and return without undue harm. If not, the banishment would stand.

But once more, he came back to the same problem. There was no possible way to police the whole frontier. DuBois could do as he pleased, anywhere out of sight of the fort. Any order of this sort was completely unenforceable.

He was considering another approach. Soldiers were sometimes punished for minor infractions by confinement for a few days. A guardhouse had been under construction when they left the fort, and was probably finished by now. A few days behind bars on bread and water might be appropriate. Yes, quite appropriate. DuBois was apparently an enjoyer of animal pleasures . . . food, brandy, women . . . yes! He would have to consider how *long* a sentence.

LeFever was pleased with himself over having found a solution to his dilemma. He was so much more relaxed that his change of mood was quite noticeable. The soldiers, seeing their officer in a better mood, were grateful. Whatever the cause, it was better than the tense silence. They began to talk and joke and resume the good-natured banter that was more characteristic.

The shadow of gloom still hung over the voyageurs, however. Their leader was still glum and quiet. It did not seem appropriate to resume jovial relations with the soldiers and traders. So they remained aloof, drawing away from any contact that might produce an unpleasant reaction from DuBois. They camped a little apart, at their own fires, and there was little conversation beyond the minimal talk needed for the conduct of travel.

Sentries were posted by the soldiers, and the voyageurs, not fully trusted, were not included in this duty, so yet another division separated the two groups. The soldiers resented that they must stand guard duty while the voyageurs slept. The voyageurs, on the other hand, reveled in the lack of military restriction that freed them from such responsibility. But it was a bittersweet satisfaction. The pleasure of a night's sleep did not quite overcome the knowledge of the reason for their exclusion. They were outsiders, not trusted. Many of them would have gladly taken their turn at sentry duty, to have been accepted with trust.

In the next few nights, a pattern of routine emerged. It was presumed that, although no pursuit had developed, any major danger would present itself from upstream. A double guard was posted there, with only one on the downstream side, the side toward "home." The voyageurs too, with no real decision having taken place, camped downstream from the soldiers.

"Sergeant," noted a sentry on the second night, "the voyageurs are a hundred paces away. Do I post *beyond* them?"

The two men walked to the other part of the camp, circled away from the river, and back. The sergeant considered.

"No," he said finally, "you post here, between the two camps. I do not want you so far from our bivouac. Let them post their own perimeter if they like!"

Once established, this pattern quickly seemed logical. No one knew, or cared, whether the voyageurs were posting a sentry on their downstream perimeter. There seemed little use for guard duty anyway. There was still no pursuit. They were camping in uninhabited places. The only real danger would be from a curious bear, perhaps, and they were easily frightened away. The entire mood of the expedition began to lighten.

The travelers began to notice the change in the country, the greener grass on the hills. They passed the heron rookery, and saw increasing evidence that here there was greater rainfall. Trees grew tall and lush along the smaller tributaries whose mouths they passed. Once more, after a time of strife, anxiety, and hardship, the expedition was becoming almost pleasant. This was reflected in the good humor of most of the party.

Even the voyageurs seemed to brighten some. They did not mingle yet, but it was obvious that their differences were waning. It began to seem that much of the strife and distrust might heal by the time they reached the fort.

All this was apparent to White Fox and his family. Though they could not fully understand the talk, they could sense the changing mood. Perhaps better than the French, even.

Red Horse sought out Paint.

"Do you think it is time to tell Blue Jacket what I saw?" he inquired.

The negro smiled. Even he was beginning to relax.

"No, no," he answered. "It seems not to matter now, Horse. Let us go. The captain will handle it."

"What will he do to Black Beard?"

"I do not know . . . a few days in the guardhouse, maybe."

"Guardhouse?"

There it was again, the language problem. There were no such words in the tongue of the People. Paint chuckled.

"Yes . . . let me . . . well, Horse, it is like a cage, for people."

"You put people in *cages?*"

He had seen, at the fort, pens of poultry and pigs, but *people?*

"Yes," Paint said cautiously. This boy asked so many questions.

"But Paint, you are a prisoner, all your life, but are not in a cage. Not even tied!"

Red Horse was using a mixture of sign-talk and French.

"No, that is different," Paint answered, in the same mix.

"Then who . . . the French put themselves in cages?"

"No . . . Horse, what would your people do to someone to punish him? For disobeying."

Red Horse thought for a moment.

"But he would not disobey."

"No, someone always might. What is there that your people are forbidden to do?"

"Like eating bear meat?" Horse asked.

"Yes, maybe . . . What would be done to him?"

"Nothing. It is his problem. The bad luck falls on him."

Paint shook his head.

"A bad choice to talk of, Horse. Now, let me . . . wait, you have a council . . . what do they decide?"

"Oh . . . where to camp. Where to hunt."

"Yes, now maybe we get somewhere. They might decide *not* to hunt?"

"Of course. The time might not be right. The holy man, my father, talks to the chiefs, and they decide."

"What if it is not the right time?"

"The herds might be driven away, and there would be hunger."

"Ah, yes! But if someone hunts anyway?"

"*Aiee!* He puts the band in danger!"

"And what is done to him?"

"The council decides. Probably drive him away, maybe for a season."

Paint was delighted.

"Yes! That is your people's punishment. That of the French is the cage!"

"I see."

He did not, fully, but it was clearer now than before. He remembered that White Fox was said to have been in a Spanish cage in Santa Fe during that war when he was a boy. That was something else, he supposed. Well, this would be interesting to see. He would ask his father about it too.

20

>> >> >>

No one was really ready for the shock that came that summer morning. Least of all Captain LeFever. Things had been going well. The travel was easy, the river's current now helping the canoemen considerably. It was not necessary to exert much power. The stream provided motion, and the steersmen only guided the vessels. Another few "sleeps," as their native companions quaintly put it, and they would be home. Well, not home, but to the fort. Somehow that goal now carried utmost importance.

Day was just dawning, and the camp was beginning to come awake. Men were rolling from their blankets, and stumbling sleepily out of the camp area a little way to urinate. LeFever lay there a moment, gathering his thoughts, and watching the interesting patterns of light and dark in the green canopy overhead. It was a beautiful grove in which they camped, very pleasant to the senses. With a feeling of satisfaction, he sat up and drew in a couple of deep breaths of cool morning air. There was a thin mist of fog on the stream, hanging in layers among the trees. A beautiful effect. The sun would soon burn off the wisps of fog, but for the moment it provided a rare sight for the travelers on the river.

A couple of soldiers approached.

"Captain," the sergeant said in a worried tone, "the voyageurs! They are gone!"

"*Gone?* What . . . how?"

"I don't know, sir. Robideaux, here, was on sentry duty, and he heard nothing."

"Heard *nothing?*" LeFever almost shouted. "Were you asleep, soldier?"

"No, sir," the trembling soldier protested. "I think not . . . I was at my post."

"We will consider this later," the captain said grimly, "but for now, tell me . . ."

"Sir, I saw that it was near dawn. The sky to the east turns a little gray, you know, before it begins . . ."

"Get on with it!" snapped LeFever.

"Yes, sir. It was near dawn . . . I heard the men getting up, going outside the camp to . . ."

"Yes?"

"Well, I noticed there was no stirring in the other camp. But I'd seen them and their fires, all night. Big fires. So I came and told the sergeant."

LeFever was already striding toward the abandoned camp. It was true. There were only the ashes of burned-out fires. Very cleverly laid fires, to be sure. They had been banked with wood in a long line, burning from west to east as new fuel was ignited through the night. The gray ash told the story. A pile of kindling to blaze up brightly from time to time, followed by a succession of larger sticks and dead limbs. The alternating bright blaze and slower heavy wood had given the impression, from a distance, that the fires were tended.

"Is their canoe missing?" he asked.

"Yes, sir, not a trace. All their baggage, too."

Well, thought LeFever, *they would not have gone back upstream. And, since they took the canoe, they are still on the river. Unless they cast it adrift and went overland. No, they would not do that . . . it would limit their options.*

"They have gone downriver," he concluded, aloud.

And judging from the ashes of the misleading fires, they had been gone most of the night. They would be nearly a day's travel ahead by this time. But *why?* This would require some thought, but it must be that the renegade DuBois had an urgent reason to reach Fort de Chastaigne well ahead of the party. The suspicion about friends in high political places recurred to him. If DuBois reached the outskirts of civilization first, his story would be believed. And what would he tell? The possibilities were frightening. It would undoubtedly be quite uncomplimentary to the commandant, possibly even damaging. If the man did have friends in high places, it could be disastrous to the career of a young officer. They must hurry to prevent what damage they could.

"Load the canoes, sergeant," LeFever said. "As fast as possible. We must catch them!"

The bewildered sergeant turned away. Why? Good riddance, it seemed to him. He had not trusted the voyageurs anyway, and was glad to see them gone.

LeFever pushed the expedition to top speed, the canoemen paddling with the current instead of merely drifting. He knew that he had little chance to overtake the renegades, but hoped to give them little time to do mischief at the fort. Though he trusted his adjutant, the lieutenant was inexperienced. What, for instance, if DuBois came in to report that the captain and his exploring party were all dead? Lieutenant Prudhomme might make decisions far differently if he were actually commandant of the fort, instead of temporarily in charge.

They traveled through that night, but LeFever realized that the effort was unrewarding. It was necessary to slow the pace during the hours of darkness, to avoid accidents. There were shoals and gravel bars that could rip the bottom out of a canoe. When morning came, everyone was exhausted from lack of sleep and the extra exertion. Impatiently the captain settled for a slower pace, and promised that they would stop for the night.

Even so, he rankled under the limitations

placed on his party. He knew that somewhere downriver the renegade DuBois was enjoying his success in escaping. Perhaps a half-day's journey, or a full day, there was no way to tell. For that matter, they could be just around the next bend of the river. Another reason, LeFever realized in retrospect, *not* to go rushing at full speed into the unknown.

Impatient, he settled down to the pace imposed on him by circumstances.

There was much about all this that was not well understood by the People from the plains. To White Fox, this had initially appeared a pleasant summer's trip to new country, a good experience for Red Horse in his learning years. But nothing, he now realized, is ever quite as simple as it seems.

He still felt a little resentment that the secondary purpose of the expedition, the search for the route to Santa Fe, had not been revealed to him from the first. If it had been explained, things would have been much easier. He could have told the captain, and avoided much travel on the wrong route. He could understand, of course. Blue Jacket had not known him, and had no reason to trust him with secret information. The captain *had* shared the expedition's secondary purpose when he felt confident in his guide. Yes, White Fox would forgive him that. Besides, Fox liked the captain. He appeared to be a good leader.

What Fox did not understand was the political infighting that was evident between the captain and the black-bearded voyageur. It was enough to know that such things do happen, and that each tribe will have its own political structure and its own problems. The friction had been evident, though not voiced aloud.

Then, whatever had happened at the Mandan village had burst the situation wide open. It had looked quite dangerous there for a few moments. It appeared that Black Beard had offended their hosts greatly. A fight over a woman, it seemed. The voyageur had nearly killed a man, who still might not recover, and then *did* kill another, in plain view of the whole town. It was understandable that the Mandans were upset. Fox had fully expected pursuit, in view of the serious nature of Black Beard's assaults.

There was something else about that whole episode. Something that had to do with Red Horse. The young man had acted strangely ever since that skirmish at the Mandan town. White Fox had watched him, and had spoken of it to South Wind. She felt it too, but neither of them could tell what was bothering their son.

Fox had assumed initially that the young man had been interested in a Mandan girl. In fact, he was certain of that, because he had noticed the girl himself, and seen the exchange of glances. *Well*, he had thought to himself, *the boy does have an eye for beauty.*

He gathered that something had gone wrong with that tryst, however. At least, the glum face and the disinterest in the rest of the world were quite unlike Red Horse's usual disposition. And the depression had not been noticeable until after that evening. Somehow White Fox had the idea that the boy's moodiness had something to do with the trouble over Black Beard. He did not see how. The woman over whom Black Beard had fought, if it really was a fight, was not the same one who had shown interest in flirting with Horse.

But there was something there. Red Horse, even in his preoccupation, still seemed to watch Black Beard from time to time. There was a look of fear, somehow. More of a fear, even, than one would have from watching the shooting. Had something happened between the two? Surely, Horse would have told them. Even more puzzling, as White Fox had quietly watched day after day, was the fact that Black Beard seemed completely unaware. *Ah, then,* Fox finally concluded, *it is something that Black Beard does not know.* Could the boy have seen something, unknown to Black Beard? Yes, that must be it! But what, and why did Red Horse fear him? At this point Fox always came to a complete stop in his logic. He could reason no further.

He wondered if Horse was confiding his problem to his black friend, Paint. He hoped so. That had been a good thing for the boy this summer.

He also knew that, when the time was right, Horse would discuss the matter with his father. He must be patient.

But then, this new development. The voyageurs had crept away in the night. There must be more to the politics of this than there appeared. At any rate, Blue Jacket seemed much more angered than one would have thought. Then he remembered. The voyageurs would reach the fort first. He did not know what might be the problem between them and the captain, but even so, he could see that such a man was not to be trusted. Yes, Blue Jacket was right to hurry!

21
>> >> >>

There were no further incidents. The travel continued smoothly, and in a few days the entire situation seemed much more relaxed. Captain LeFever realized that a time of reckoning must come. Yet, as they traveled on the river, it was difficult to worry. The fine weather held, and there was nothing to mar enjoyment of the magnificent scenery, the rocky bluffs and long vistas of forest or prairie. He could deal with his problems, especially that of DuBois, when they arrived at the fort. His confidence grew. There, at Fort de Chastaigne, he would be in his own domain, on his own terms. The decisions that at one time seemed to present a major dilemma now appeared quite simple.

One man was involved, the voyageur DuBois. There was no other leader among the voyageurs who would challenge the authority of the military. He would remove DuBois and his problems would be behind him. Actually, he now realized, he could completely avoid the final decision. He would merely arrest the voyageur and transfer him, in irons, to the next higher command. That would neatly sidestep the risk of stepping on political toes. If there was an influential person somewhere who would defend DuBois, so be it. LeFever would have done his duty in calling attention to the problem. Then, let the chips fall where they may! He, LeFever, would be in no trouble for referring it up the chain of command. At worst, DuBois would be released to return and again become a nuisance. At best, he would be imprisoned.

Yes, as he thought about it, the captain was pleased even more with the manner in which his problems were resolving. In his mind, he began to compose the letter that he would send with the prisoner back to the territorial governor.

There was another letter to write, too. It had been so long, so frustrating, to be apart from Collette. They had planned marriage after his tour of duty at this frontier post. This was to be his great opportunity, the establishment of his own fort on the edge of the wilderness. There were two possibilities that he had seen. Either would make him ready, professionally, for the responsibilities of a wife and family. His expertise might be noticed, as Fort de Chastaigne was skillfully administered, and he might be chosen for rapid promotion. That would bring Collette a great deal of pride, being transferred to higher posts.

The other possibility had begun to look even

brighter. The colony at the fort was rapidly becoming self-sustaining. The gardens and crops were growing properly, at least at the time the expedition left. A good season would firmly establish the colony. The livestock had wintered well. It had begun to appear that a thriving fur trade was possible.

If, in addition to this stable community, he could manage contact and trade with the Spanish in Santa Fe . . . well, the world was his. He could stay right there in the heartland, based at de Chastaigne, and grow with the new country. He might do well, he now daydreamed, to consider asking for a political appointment as governor, when the time came. The prestige and honor that he could offer Collette, the governor's wife!

Either way, he thought, it was time they married. He would write immediately to bring her here. He had lived alone long enough, and he needed her to share his thoughts and dreams, as well as his bed. Maybe . . . he hoped that there would be a letter waiting at the fort for him. Surely there would. He had not heard from her for several months. Communication was slow, but yes, he should have her letter, waiting for him.

He began to look forward, more each day, to their arrival at the fort. It seemed that everything good was destined to begin at that time. Of course, there was the exploration for the route to Santa Fe. But first things first. The arrest, the letters, and he must consult with White Fox. Would there be time to go to Santa Fe yet this season? He could ask White Fox about that even before they arrived at the fort. He thought that it would be possible, but it should be carefully planned. By horseback, Fox had said. They could buy horses from the natives. Fox's people were noted for their horses, it seemed. What were they sometimes called? "Elk-dog People," the medicine man had said. Of course, the Kenzas possessed some horses. Well, the journey could be planned very quickly, and he would do so immediately.

All in all, LeFever's confidence was returning rapidly as they neared the fort. His old enthusiasm for a challenge was rising, and he was ready to start.

The canoes rounded the last bend, and he saw the fort ahead in the distance. It was a peaceful scene. The cows grazed on their island pasture, and smoke curled lazily from one of the chimneys in the fort itself. He had doubted that chimneys built that way could be made to work without danger of burning. There had been a scarcity of stone, and the Kenzas had suggested this technique. The fireplaces themselves were of stone, but above the shelving mantle the chimneys were of sticks, laid like a log house and heavily plastered with clay inside and out. The heat from the fireplace had baked the clay flue, making it hard and impervious to weather. It would need replacing, of course, after a few seasons. But materials for repair were easily available.

Obviously, he noted, the method was successful. There was a homelike atmosphere about the
entire pastoral scene that made it seem a real
homecoming. His daydream of bringing his bride
here seemed perfectly reasonable.

He was proud of the things he had accomplished. He could see as they turned in to shore
that the construction had proceeded under the direction of Lieutenant Prudhomme. The roofs of
structures that had been barely started now
loomed above the palisade.

The canoe grounded and he stepped out, striding up the slope with determination. He was only
halfway to the palisade when his adjutant came
out of the gate, smiling broadly.

"Welcome home, Captain!"

"Thank you, Jacque. I see construction has
gone well."

"Yes, sir. The powder magazine is finished, one
of the other . . ."

"Never mind now, Lieutenant. There are other
things . . . I want DuBois put in irons."

"Who?" asked the astonished adjutant.

"Baptiste DuBois. I want him arrested at once."

"The voyageur, Captain? What has he done?"

"I will tell you all about it, Jacque, but first, let
us do it. Now, where is he?"

The astonished look still hung unchecked on
Lieutenant Prudhomme's face.

"Why . . . I . . . Captain, he is not here! I
have not seen the man since before you left!"

Anger swept over LeFever.

"Nonsense!" he snorted. "We were . . ." He paused, trying to organize his thoughts as the calm pastoral tone of the scene vanished like a burst bubble. "We were traveling on the river together," he said calmly. "They came on ahead. He is not here?"

"No, sir," the bewildered lieutenant protested, "the voyageurs . . . you know how they come and go!"

"But a canoe of them? Some six or eight? And probably not more than two days ago?"

"Of course, Captain . . . maybe two or three canoes. Look, there are some now . . . downstream. More over there . . . What has happened?"

Still fighting his anger, LeFever quickly sketched in the story. Now he was quite suspicious. DuBois *was* up to something. There must have been a reason for the voyageur's rush to get home well ahead of the soldiers.

"Look!" LeFever cried suddenly, "that man, the thin one in the red cap! He was with DuBois!"

He pointed to a group of voyageurs squatting around a fire some fifty paces from the fort. The two officers walked across the open area to approach them.

"What is your name?" LeFever demanded of the man in the red wool cap.

"Bonet, m'sieur, Pierre Bonet."

"Yes. Now, Bonet, you were with us on the river, no?"

"Of course, m'sieur. Also Louis, there, as well as André."

LeFever smiled benignly, trying to remain calm.

"Yes. I remember you. But where is DuBois?"

"DuBois, m'sieur? Baptiste DuBois?"

Of course, you idiot, thought LeFever, *who else would I mean?*

Aloud, he remained cordial.

"Yes, that one."

"Ah, I have not seen him."

"Not seen him? But you were with him!"

The little man spread his hands in mock consternation.

"Of course, m'sieur. I thought you meant today."

You lie, thought LeFever. *No one is this stupid.* He tried a new approach.

"When did you reach the fort?"

"Yesterday, m'sieur. You meant *yesterday?*"

"Yes. Was DuBois with you when you reached the fort yesterday?"

The voyageurs looked at each other in serious doubt.

"I think so, Captain. Is it not, André?"

The other man, a short, weasel-faced individual with pockmarked cheeks, nodded.

"It is so, Captain."

"Then where is he now?"

Again, the infuriating looks of innocence were exchanged all around.

"He is not here, m'sieur," Bonet said seriously.

"I can see that," snapped LeFever.

He would have liked to toss the lot of them in irons. He knew they were laughing at him, aware of his frustration and his inability to do anything about it. They were much more intelligent than they seemed, and were protecting their leader. He must remain calm.

"If you see him, tell him I want to talk to him," he said casually as he turned away.

He was all but certain that he heard a muffled snicker behind him. Where had the man gone? More important, *why?* DuBois must know that he could only delay the reckoning, not avoid it. What did he hope to gain by delay?

LeFever and Prudhomme started back toward the fort.

"Anything important happen?" asked LeFever.

"No . . . oh, a courier from the governor, but no new orders. He came mostly to bring mail from home. One for you . . . woman's handwriting. Collette, maybe?" he teased.

"Maybe."

Well, he would read that letter, and then maybe write one to Collette. That would help, while he tried to figure out what sort of scheme DuBois was up to. Certainly there was a scheme. At any rate, they were back at the fort now. Whatever the scheme might be, the next move would be the voyageur's. He would have to wait and see.

22
>> >> >>

The next morning White Fox was summoned for a council with the captain. At least, thought LeFever, here was something he could do. Plans could be made for the Santa Fe exploration, even while they waited for DuBois's next move.

LeFever had decided to postpone writing his fiancée. Not that he was disinterested. He longed for her more than ever. There had been a letter, as Lieutenant Prudhomme had suggested. Collette had filled the pages with descriptions of her girlish social activities, and gossipy news of their friends and acquaintances. At one time these things would have been a major part of his world. Now they seemed silly and of no consequence. Here in the stark realism of the frontier, it was hard to remember a world where the most important event of the day was the quality of Emily Bordeau's crepes.

For a page and a half at the end of the letter, however, Collette had poured out her heart. It was apparent that her feelings were as strong as ever, her longing for him as great.

My Charles, I long to be with you. Until then, all my love,

Your Collette

A lump rose in his throat as he finished the page, and he glanced quickly around to be sure he was unobserved as he folded the letter and slipped it into the breast pocket of his tunic.

He heard the approach of the orderly who had been sent to bring White Fox. He hastened to straighten his uniform and compose his facial expression into that of a stoic leader of men.

"*Ah-koh,* my chief," greeted White Fox. "What is your wish?"

"Ah, yes, Fox. I wanted to ask about the route to Santa Fe."

He unfurled a crude map on the desk, and held it in place with an inkwell and a box of blotting sand.

"Now here," he pointed, "is the fort. This is the river where we were. Now, where is this southwest trail?"

White Fox studied the paper for a little while.

"My friend," he said finally, "I do not know of such things. This is much like our story-skins, but the marks mean little to me. How is it . . . ?"

"Of course. Forgive me!" LeFever said. "You have not seen maps. Let me show you. This mark, the circle with points at the top and sides . . . shows the directions. The longest point is North."

"Ah, yes . . . the arrow points to the Real-star."

"Well . . . yes, that is true."

"But we were on the river, here, many sleeps. How can it show all?"

LeFever thought a moment. If they traveled about so many furlongs in a day . . .

"This is a very small picture," he explained. "We traveled about this far in a day." He placed a mark on the map to indicate a day's travel, then others to show the Mandan towns. "Here is the farthest upstream, where we were."

White Fox nodded.

"And this line . . . this river, is the River of the Kenzas?"

"Yes, yes!" LeFever was excited at Fox's quick understanding. "Is that where the trail follows? The Southwest Trail you told of?"

"No, there is another river, to the south, here. The *Ar-kenzas*, it is called . . . 'Below-the-Kenzas' . . . the trail follows that river."

"Yes . . . Fox, can we travel to Santa Fe before winter?"

"Maybe so. We need horses."

"We can get horses from the Kenzas."

"Yes, but . . . Blue Jacket, they are not as good as the horses of my people."

"Could we trade for horses with your tribe?"

"Of course . . . ride Kenza horses that far, and then trade?"

"Yes! Would some of your people go with us? Some warriors?"

"Maybe so. Some would be proud to do this."

"Good!"

"When did you wish to go?" White Fox asked. "Tomorrow?"

"No . . . I . . ."

LeFever had not considered this. He could not leave until, in some manner or other, the matter of the voyageur, DuBois, had been resolved. What if the man had simply started back to civilization? And how would they ever know? Once more, the frustration of the entire situation descended on him.

"My chief," Fox spoke unexpectedly, "what of the Black Beard, DuBois?"

Once more, LeFever was startled at the deep insight of this man of the prairie. Fox had correctly observed that this matter must be resolved before the captain could leave again.

"It is true," he admitted openly. "I must find him, Fox. He must answer for the killing upriver."

"Find him? But he is here, my chief!"

"Here?" asked the astonished LeFever. "At de Chastaigne?"

"Yes, of course. The Kenzas have seen him . . . they asked us what happened upstream."

Of course . . . the native grapevine! How

quickly it spread the news. He must learn to use it to better advantage.

"Fox," he asked, "could you find out where he is staying, without letting him know?"

"Maybe so."

"I want you to try. This is important to our search for Santa Fe."

"Yes, I will try."

"Good. Now, before you go, look at this map again. Can you show me about where the Arkenzas would be?"

"Of course. About here." He pointed.

"Good. Now, the mountains?"

"Your story-skin is not big enough. About here, off the skin."

"That far? Then where is Santa Fe?"

"Off the skin too. About here, much south. There are two ways."

"*Two* trails?"

"No, one trail. It goes to the mountains, over a pass called *Raton.* But there is a branch, across the desert . . . it is shorter."

"Can we use it?"

White Fox considered.

"Maybe not. We can ask some of the old people. They have made that trip. But at this season, I think not. There is no water."

"There is water, sometimes?"

"Spring, maybe. Not now."

LeFever was mentally regretting, once more, that he had not been able to take fuller advantage of the experience and expertise of this man. But how could he have known? He realized that he was barely beginning to see the possibilities, the things one could learn from these people of the heartland.

"We will ask some men who have used it," concluded White Fox.

The two stood, still looking at the map.

"Could you help me draw some of these things?" LeFever asked.

"There is no room on the skin!"

LeFever smiled.

"On another 'skin,' maybe?"

"Maybe so. We can mark how far is one sleep, no?"

The conversation was interrupted by a loud, reverberating explosion. It seemed very near at hand. White Fox, unaccustomed to such noises, recoiled impulsively. LeFever, nearly as surprised, recognized the boom of a musket. From the sound, he judged it must have been right there, within the enclosure of the compound. An unforgivable carelessness, to fire a musket accidently there, putting many people, including women and children, in danger. He dashed outside.

People were running, yelling, trying to determine what was happening.

"Are we being attacked?" someone screamed in terror.

LeFever encountered his sergeant.

"What is happening?" he asked.

"I do not know, Captain. The shot came from the trader's."

The two ran in that direction, shouldering through the crowd. LeFever looked through the open doorway.

"Get back, Captain. Back, or I kill her!" A slurred voice called from inside.

It took a moment for his eyes to adjust to the dimness inside, and a moment longer to evaluate the situation. A soldier, staggering and apparently quite drunk, held the trader's wife in his left arm, crushing her tightly against him. In his other hand there was a knife, held just barely touching the creamy skin of Madeline LaFontaine's throat. The seductive blue eyes with their long lashes now reflected only terror. She opened her mouth to scream, and the soldier pressed the knife point a little harder against her skin.

"You be quiet!" the soldier hissed.

"Yes! Don't hurt me," the woman pleaded.

The knife, LeFever noted, was the long, slim fighting knife of the Paris streets. Sharp as a razor, such a weapon could do tremendous damage with one stroking slash. From the way this man held it, LeFever was certain that he was an expert with such a knife.

"Soldier," he called, "let us talk. What is your name?"

The soldier laughed, a drunken laugh of scorn.

"What difference, Captain? You never knew it before. And what is there to talk of? I killed him, and I will kill this whore too, if you don't back off."

Killed who? LeFever thought. He glanced around the room. Then through the doorway to the little bedroom behind, he saw the lifeless form on the floor. LaFontaine, just beginning his trading career on the frontier, would trade no more. The musket ball had torn away the side of his face, and a great puddle of blood seemed to be still growing on the rough plank floor. The soldier's musket lay near the body. Once fired, it was of little use until reloaded, and there had been no time.

It was easy to surmise what had happened. The little tart had carried her flirtations too far, and this soldier, under the influence of drink, had taken advantage of the invitation. The trader had arrived at an inopportune moment, and had been struck down . . . A woman such as this could always bring trouble, LeFever thought.

"Look, soldier, put down the knife," he pleaded.

"No! What chance would I have then? You will not harm me as long as I have this woman!"

His voice was thick with brandy, but his logic was accurate. There was nothing that anyone could do without risking the woman's life.

"Back off, now!" the soldier yelled. "We are coming out."

He shifted his encircling arm to circle the woman's neck, and half dragged her toward the doorway. The knife's point still touched her exposed throat.

"Back," LeFever called to the crowd. "Get back. No one is to try to stop him!"

It would be too dangerous. Give the idiot whatever he wanted, for now. Try not to lose another life. Sooner or later the man must sleep. And after all, there was really no place he could go.

23
»»» »» »»

"**B**ack," called LeFever to the gathering crowd. "Everyone get back!"

He must be cautious now. Any threat, or even anything seen as a threat by the soldier, could be fatal to the hostage. He spoke again.

"Where do you want to go?"

The soldier seemed confused for a moment. He was possibly too drunk to think efficiently. The terrified woman began to whimper again.

"Quiet!" her captor snarled. "You be still, now!"

Roughly, he jerked the arm around her neck a time or two, to show his authority.

"I am coming out, Captain," he called. "If anyone tries to stop me, I'll slit her throat!"

"Yes, I know." The captain raised his voice, shouting to the crowd. "No one is to try to stop this man!"

The order was more for the benefit of the crazed soldier. No one seemed to have any desire to interfere. The captain's main concern was that someone might try to shoot the man from a little distance. That would be quite dangerous to the prisoner. She might be struck by the shot . . . the muskets of the troops were imprecise in their accuracy, at best. A second danger would be that the blow of the musket ball would not kill instantly. It was a heavy lead projectile, but traveled at relatively slow speed. It was often possible to catch a glimpse of the ball in flight. If it struck, even fatally, there could still be the space of a heartbeat or two when a quick stroke of the knife . . . it would take so little to drain the life from that delicate throat. Even a convulsive dying shudder of the knife-wielding arm.

The soldier was edging toward the doorway now, blinking stupidly in the bright light of day. Madeline LaFontaine's face was chalk-white, her eyes filled with terror. Very slowly, the soldier and his hostage edged past Captain LeFever.

"Help me!" the woman pleaded in a voice that was no more than a whisper.

"Shut up!" her captor snarled.

Step by step, with agonizing slowness, the two slid out the door. The man placed his back to the logs of the cabin and began to side-step to his right along the wall. He felt his way cautiously, with hips and shoulders sliding along the rough logs of the structure.

He reached the corner of the house and stopped, glancing around in confusion for a moment. His plan was apparently quite ill formed, not reaching past this point. To go beyond this corner would expose his back, unless he followed the wall around, which would seem to be a useless exercise, leading nowhere. His glance fell on the newly finished structure a short distance away. No more than a step or two . . . yes! Quickly, he dragged his terrified hostage across the intervening space and leaned against the wall of the new building.

With a sinking feeling LeFever realized that this was the powder magazine. At a post of this size, powder storage was not of major importance. Quantities of gunpowder on hand at any given time would be limited to two or three kegs. It was for security that LeFever had ordered its construction. Extra heavy logs had been used, and special care to provide a leak-proof roof. The magazine was only three paces square, and its heavy plank door was secured with an iron hasp and a heavy lock. There were no windows. LeFever was proud of this accomplishment, a businesslike military installation.

As the renegade soldier felt his way along the wall, LeFever saw with dismay that the lock was open, hanging through the slot of the hasp. At most times it would have been locked, but now . . . the adjutant had been issuing powder, and . . . LeFever hoped against hope that the fugitive would not notice.

There was no such luck. Even in his drunken

state, the soldier noticed LeFever's attention to
the door behind him. He glanced down, for only
an instant, and smiled. He pushed the door with
his hip and it creaked open, exposing the dark
interior of the little structure. He backed into the
room, dragging the woman.

"No, not the magazine, soldier!" LeFever
pleaded.

"Why not, Captain?" the man chortled in tri-
umph. "This gives me high card, no?"

"You cannot eat or drink powder."

"But I can blow it up! I have flint and steel!"

"And then you would be dead."

"It does not matter. If I surrender to you, I am
dead anyway."

"The woman?"

"She is dead too, unless you do as I say."

He took out a flint and steel, relinquishing his
knife for a moment. He held them up, in plain
view.

"Now, Captain," he said, spitting the word
"Captain" as if it were an oath, "I am finished
talking. Get those people away from here. I want
some supplies, ready to carry."

LeFever turned.

"Lieutenant! Sergeant! Clear the fort! Everyone
outside the wall!"

He was only too happy to do this. If that
drunken idiot happened to strike a spark . . .
even an accident, like dropping his flint and steel,
might set off a blast that would level the fort. His

skin prickled at the thought that he must stay here to try to negotiate until an opportunity came to kill or overpower this maniac. He could clearly see, behind the two figures in the hut, the kegs of powder. One was open; the lieutenant must have been in the process of measuring and issuing . . . Damn that Prudhomme, to leave such a task unattended. He would see to that sort of negligence after this was over. If they survived, of course.

People were hurrying out the gate of the stockade, casting anxious glances at the powder house. A little child cried, and the mother tried to hush it.

"Sergeant, get this man a pack of supplies, ready for travel."

This order was more for the benefit of the fugitive than anyone else. He must make the man believe that his escape was possible. At the same time, he had no intention of allowing the soldier to escape. The man must be captured and tried, if possible. If not . . .

"I have ordered your supplies," he called. "Now let the woman go."

The soldier laughed, a mirthless laugh.

"You think I am crazy? She is the only reason I am still alive now!"

Well, the man was sober enough to realize that fact. It was rapidly becoming a stalemate. There were still a handful of people moving toward the gate. Some apparently did not realize the gravity of the situation, and were dawdling. One woman turned back for a child's doll. Others paused to stare curiously.

"Outside! Hurry, outside the stockade!" LeFever shouted. "Everyone!"

From the corner of his eye, LeFever saw the hint of motion. Around the corner of one of the other buildings came a familiar figure, a hulking figure with a black beard. *DuBois!* What the hell was he doing here?

The voyageur walked straight forward, stepping up beside LeFever.

"Get back!" the captain yelled at him. "Outside the fort! What are you doing here?"

DuBois did not answer. The captain saw that in his right hand the voyageur carried a small ax . . . the throwing-ax so widely used in the area where they had previously been stationed. It was a favorite weapon of the woodlands.

DuBois's arm rose as he took a stance.

"Put it down!" screamed the fugitive in the hut. "I'll . . ."

There was a moment of indecision, LeFever saw as he turned back to look inside. The soldier had put his knife aside to threaten with the flint and steel, but now . . . It was unclear whether he intended to reach for the knife or attempt to strike the deadly spark. As it turned out, there was time for neither. The throwing ax flew, hard and swift, turning over in the air, the lighter handle describing a circle around the heavier blade. The blade was forward again when it struck, a sickening, thwacking sound on muscle and bone. There was only an instant when the weapon could be seen jutting from the blue-jacketed right shoulder of the fugitive. He was knocked backward, losing his grip on his hostage and falling heavily over a powder keg.

"Run! Run!" LeFever yelled at the woman.

Terrified, she managed to scramble to her feet and run. With skirts lifted and legs flying, she sprinted past the two men and on toward the group of stragglers at the gate.

LeFever turned back toward the magazine. The soldier had rolled over on his belly, facing the doorway, and was wallowing around on the floor. LeFever stepped forward to put the man into custody. It was over.

Blood gushed from the wounded shoulder, the arm hanging useless at his side. It would be unusual, LeFever thought, if the man lived long enough to stand trial. The soldier struggled to his knees, and now LeFever saw for the first time that he had drawn a pistol from his belt with his left hand. The troops were not issued pistols, so he must have stolen it from the trader, thought LeFever. It was ludicrous, he realized even in the moment of the emergency, to wonder where the weapon had come from.

The soldier, on his knees, was attempting to set the cock with his left thumb, and LeFever was about to rush forward to grab the weapon. How loud it seemed, the tiny double click that told him the weapon was set and ready to fire. The soldier raised and pointed the pistol, not at LeFever, but past him, at the burly form of Du-Bois, outside. Horrified, LeFever realized that it did not matter where the gun was aimed. If he fired it, there would be a shower of sparks when the flint struck the frizzen. There was a pinch of gunpowder in the pan of the weapon, but even the main charge was tiny compared to the keg of spilled powder scattered on the floor.

"Look out!" LeFever yelled, turning for the door.

He lunged outside, turning left toward the shelter of the dead trader's house. It was only a short distance, but the time was even shorter. One step, two, three . . . it was like running in a dream, where the dreamer tries his utmost but makes almost no progress. On the fourth step he collided with the voyageur, as the two dove headfirst behind the dubious shelter of the cabin's front corner. Then the whole world seemed to explode, in a deafening roar of smoke and flame and flying timbers.

24
>> >> >>

Excellency . . .

It is my regret to report an accident at
Fort de Chastaigne. The powder magazine
was exploded by one of the troops who was
crazed by brandy. He had killed the trader,
Monsieur LaFontaine, and taken his wife as
a hostage . . .

LeFever sighed deeply and crumpled the sheet
on which he had been writing. This was his sev-
enth attempt. There was simply no way to tell
this incredible story without reflecting unfavor-
ably on his command, and on his own authority.
Every way in which he had attempted to write it
was wrong, raising questions which the governor
would not overlook.

Where, for instance, did the soldier acquire the
brandy? How did he happen to shoot the trader
(whose political connections LeFever was beginning to dread)? Why was he not immediately

placed under arrest, and how could he have taken
the trader's wife as hostage? How did he have ac-
cess to the powder house?

LeFever sighed again. His head still throbbed,
despite the brandy he had taken. He could not
hear at all from his left ear. The slight bleeding
from that ear indicated internal injury. Maybe he
would never hear again on that side. The right ear
buzzed with a ringing sound, at some times worse
than others. Even after twenty-four hours, he felt
little improvement.

The bandage around his head showed one
bright red spot over the left eye, where the bleeding had soaked through. He had not even realized
at first that he had been struck by some sort of
flying debris. He had been staggering around, confused and listening to the screams of the injured
and dying. Then he realized that blood was running down into his eyes, obscuring his vision.

In the smoky, dust-filled maelstrom after the
explosion, it had been hard to know anything
that was happening. Clouds of acrid black-powder
smoke burned lungs and eyes and initiated fits of
coughing. He could see DuBois, also staggering
blindly around in the dust and debris. There was
a patter like rain. It took a moment to realize that
it was debris, thrown high into the air by the explosion, falling back to earth.

As the smoke and dust began to clear, he could
see a crater where the magazine had stood. The
roof of the trader's house was gone, and the wall

adjacent to the vanished powder house had collapsed. He found that he was looking out through a gap in the palisade some three paces in width, at the calm of the river beyond.

As if dreaming, he remembered a massive timber from the powder magazine, whirling in a deadly spinning arc toward the gate. Four were dead there. Three soldiers, attempting to complete the evacuation, had been hurrying the civilians along. They were struck down like stalks of maize before the knife at harvest. Two of these were dead. The third, his legs mangled hopelessly would have been better off so.

A mother and her small child were also killed by the flying timbers, and there were dozens of minor injuries from falling debris. Ironically, Madeline LaFontaine, who had been at more risk than anyone for a time, was unscathed. She had darted through the crowd and was completely outside the palisade when the blast came.

LeFever and DuBois, although closer to the explosion, had been partly sheltered by the front wall of the trader's house. Their injuries were from the concussion of the blast, not from thrown debris. Their desperate leap to the scant safety of the wall had saved both men.

No trace of the remains of the drunken soldier had been found. LeFever suspected that most of the garrison did not *want* to find the sort of grisly evidence that might be there.

To the captain, perhaps the most frustrating

thing about this whole debacle was that he was now unable to arrest or discipline DuBois. When the voyageur had reappeared, the drama of the trader's murder was already in progress. And illogical as it seemed, DuBois had become the hero of the affair. He had, with unerring accuracy, thrown the ax that had allowed the escape of the hostage. Since that had been successful, the risks were now overlooked.

Damn the man! LeFever fumed to himself. That was too risky a play. If he had aimed poorly, the throat of the woman would have been slashed, causing her lifeblood to ebb in the dusky powder house. She could even have been killed if her captor had happened to jerk away from the thrown ax. It was far too risky a move, and if the attempt had ended in tragedy for the hostage, DuBois would now be in irons. But it had been successful, and DuBois was a hero. By contrast, the military, especially LeFever as commandant, had been made to appear ineffectual. Where he had failed to rescue the hostage, DuBois had succeeded.

And now he struggled to write his damned report. The whole thing, he had nearly decided, was almost too big to commit to paper. He toyed with the idea of going to the governor himself with a verbal report. Yet that would possibly appear to be leaving his post in time of crisis. Additionally, he hesitated to leave the fort with DuBois still there, still riding the crest of a hero's popularity. He still suspected that DuBois was the source of the brandy that had precipitated the tragedy.

Maybe he could send Prudhomme with a report. Still, he was displeased with the lieutenant's possible breach of protocol in leaving the powder magazine unlocked. If that was as LeFever suspected, it was possible that Prudhomme would be more concerned with justifying his own actions than giving an accurate report.

LeFever sighed again, and rose from the desk to step outside. His head reacted with a throb of pain, but he clenched his teeth and limped outside. Soldiers were working to clear the area. Splintered logs were dragged outside the palisade, being salvaged for fuel. Those timbers that appeared sound were being laid aside for use in the reconstruction. The work was going efficiently, and for a moment he felt a trace of his pride in a well-ordered command.

Possibly he could delay the report for a day or two. There were, after all, a number of loose ends and unanswered questions. What, for instance, should he recommend about the possibility of fur trade with the Mandans? There had not even been time, yet, to know where they stood on that after the incident upriver. And what of the Spanish trading venture? He must still explore that possibility.

Well, maybe after his head felt better . . . For now, it seemed expedient to defer his report. He turned back to the desk, drew out a sheet of paper, and dipped his pen once more.

> Excellency . . .
>   It is my unfortunate duty to report an
> accident at Fort de Chastaigne, with the loss of
> our powder magazine. We have suffered some
> casualties, but the situation is in hand. A more
> complete report will be forthcoming.
>   Capt. Chas. LeFever,
>   Commandant, Ft. de Chastaigne

There! That should hold the situation for the present. Quite satisfied with himself, he folded the sheet and lit a candle to melt the stick of bright red wax. Then he affixed the military seal and waved the report gently while the circle of wax hardened.

"Sergeant," he called, "I need a messenger to go to the governor." He paused a moment, and added, "Pick a closemouthed man."

"Yes, sir."

He was feeling better about the situation. Now he could begin to do something about some of those loose ends.

First he would check on the rebuilding, and go to express official condolences to the families of the dead, and to the trader's widow. Yes, and letters to next of kin of his soldiers.

He must decide, within a day or two, whether it was practical to make the try for Santa Fe this season. Tomorrow might be a better evaluation of that possibility. Meanwhile, he must talk to White Fox. He had not seen Fox since the shooting. But that project, the trail to Santa Fe, depended much on the cooperation of the medicine man from the plains.

He walked over to where the men were digging, resetting the logs of the palisade. It was going well, and he began to feel considerably better. Even his head throbbed somewhat less. He began to think of other duties that must be carried out. Powder, to replace that which was lost. The messenger had not yet departed . . . he would send a requisition with him. He turned to attend to that task.

There was one more thing, one he detested even to think about. He must have some sort of conversation with DuBois. Even though he could not exert much discipline, he must let the voyageur know of his disapproval. He would mention the distribution of brandy, or at least his suspicions, as a warning to DuBois. There would be no point in trying to question him. The man would lie anyway. He could not criticize, at least not openly, the manner in which the hostage had been freed. DuBois was receiving too much praise on that.

LeFever could, however, *thank* him for his help . . . yes! It is impossible to argue with one who agrees with you. Thank him, but comment on the *luck* involved in that success. That would let Du-

Bois know that whatever others might think, he, LeFever, disapproved, and was aware that it was a foolish move. Yes, he would go, now, and talk to the voyageur. He strode out the gate, noting the scarred and battered gateposts as he did so, and turned toward the voyageurs' camp.

Wait, he told himself. *Let him come to me!*

Turning on his heel, he reentered the palisade and walked back toward the headquarters.

"Corporal," he told the clerk at the desk, "I wish to see the voyageur, Baptiste DuBois. Send someone to bring him to my office."

25

>> >> >>

It was three days, now, since the tragedy at Fort de Chastaigne. People were returning to normal activities, although very slowly. Many were not sleeping well. It was not uncommon to wake in a panic of fear after nightmares of impending hell on earth, complete with fire and smoke.

The rebuilding was going slowly. Summer was not the proper time of year to cut new logs. Green timbers would not cure properly, and would shrink, crack, and warp badly, leading to poor construction. It had been decided to repair the palisade only, using seasoned material from the damaged structures. For the present, the shell of the trader's house remained as a reminder of the tragedy.

Ironically, the weather was idyllic. The funerals for the dead were carried out on a beautiful afternoon on the slope behind the fort. The soft summer breeze stirred the lush green of the valley, carrying scents of wildflowers. The sounds of summer were a soft hum, not even intruding on the senses. The buzz of bees, attending blossoms in the meadow; the distant call of a bird; the splash of a fish in the stream below.

It was during the letdown after the multiple funeral that Madeline LaFontaine made her way along the wooded path by the river. She was still wearing a black scarf over her head, a frontier adaptation in the absence of civilized mourning clothes. Under the watchful eyes of the entire community, she had survived the shock of abduction, the loss of her husband and home, and the difficult period of mourning.

This afternoon she had told the family with whom she was staying that she must have some time alone, to pray and meditate, to try to reorganize her life. *Poor thing,* thought her hostess, *one could forgive her for her past flirtations. She surely should not have had to endure this.*

Madeline picked her way along the path, looking a bit anxious as she did so. Finally she turned aside, pushing through a leafy screen into a little clearing. She glanced around, still uneasy, and finally walked over to sit on a log. An attentive observer might have noticed that although she appeared anxious, the woman seemed quite familiar with this place. Also, that she appeared to be waiting for something.

It was for some time that she sat, alert to every sound, every rustle of a squirrel in the leaves of the woodland floor. With the identification of each intrusion into her solitude, she would again lapse into quiet meditation.

Then came the unmistakable sounds of someone's approach. She reacted with alarm, darting quickly to a hiding place among the hazel and dogwood shrubs on the slope. She had barely vanished from sight, and the leaves had hardly settled back into place, when the boughs parted on the opposite side of the clearing. A tall, burly man strode into the open, paused, and looked around curiously. He scratched at his black beard, then finger-combed it roughly back into position. He strode the few steps across the clearing and paused beside the log, again looking searchingly around the area.

Madeline LaFontaine slipped quietly from her hiding place.

"Baptiste!" she said softly, as the voyageur gathered her in his arms. "I was not sure it was you!"

"You were expecting someone else, no?" DuBois teased.

"No, no, of course not."

The blue eyes which had been lowered in mourning for three days now shone with excitement as she looked into his face.

"Bap! It worked! We did it!"

"Yes."

His hands were caressing her body with a familiarity that told of long experience.

"I was scared, when he grabbed me, with the knife," she admitted.

"I too, little one. We did not count on that," he chuckled.

"But you saved me."

"I had to do something. That fool of a captain . . . but the powder magazine! Who would have thought of *that?*"

"It solved many problems," she observed with a pleasant little chuckle. "Everyone thinks only of that."

They paused a moment for a long and passionate kiss. Finally, she pushed gently away, though not very far.

"Stop! We must plan."

"I will *never* stop," he warned, pawing at her again.

"I mean for now, silly," she giggled, taking his hand in both of hers to remove it to his side. "Now, when do we go?"

"Tonight?"

"No, no, I must have a little time. Be decent, Bap! Jacque is hardly cold."

DuBois looked crestfallen, and to convince him of her devotion, she kissed him warmly.

"A few days, maybe," she said soothingly.

He sighed deeply.

"I have waited a long time."

"And I too, my dear. But soon, we will . . ."

He stopped her sentence with another passionate kiss and pulled her to him, drawing her close as they sank to a sitting position on the log, then slid to the ground together.

"Bap! Your beard tickles!" she giggled.

"I will shave it off, after we leave. We will be harder to recognize."

He pressed closer to her, becoming more insistent. Gently, she tried to push him away.

"No, not here . . ." she whispered.

"Yes!" he insisted. "Remember Quebec?"

She smiled dreamily.

"Well . . . yes . . ."

"It will be like that again," he promised.

"It has taken so long . . . so much planning," she mused, "and I did not even know you were at de Chastaigne."

"But, we are together, now," he whispered.

Her eyes were closed, her entire attention given to the romance of the moment. They did not speak again, and there was only the rustle of the leafy canopy overhead, and the sweet sounds of summer.

There was a slight noise, a mere diversion from the whisper of the breeze in the trees. Lazily, Madeline LaFontaine opened her eyes. To her utter horror, there was a face looking down into hers . . . the face of a tall, muscular native. He was nearly naked, and his expression radiated hatred. He was in the act of lifting a spear high overhead with both hands.

"Baptiste!" she screamed, but the voyageur did

not even have time to turn and look before the lance descended.

"Mandan." White Fox signed and spoke at the same time. "Come, we will tell Blue Jacket."

Red Horse stood, unable to tear his eyes from the sight. He had discovered the dead couple, still locked in embrace, and had run to bring his father. It was an unbelievably inappropriate thing, the shaft of the lance sticking up through the two bodies, pointing at the sky above and driven into the earth beneath them. The clear blue eyes, now dry and crusted in death, stared sightlessly. Even now, there was a hint of surprise and terror in the lifeless face. To one side lay her black scarf.

"Father . . . who?"

"Mandan," repeated White Fox. "The lance."

"Why did he not take his weapon?"

"He wanted it to be found. To tell who did this."

"Like the Head Splitters, when they mark a kill to tell that they did it?"

"Yes, like that."

"But *who?*"

Even as he spoke the question, it was apparent that Red Horse had reasoned it out.

"Yes . . . I see. Father, this was the man whose wife was taken at the village . . ."

"Yes," agreed White Fox. "It must be the man you told me of, the one who was stabbed. He recovered, and came looking for Black Beard. Or, it could be of the family of the man who was shot."

Red Horse nodded. It was apparent that a man like Black Beard would have many enemies. It was enough for the killer to know that it would be recognized as a Mandan deed of vengeance by those who discovered it.

"Come, we will tell Blue Jacket," White Fox repeated.

"What? Both of them?" LeFever gasped.

The trader's wife, now his widow, had been missing since just before dark last evening. No one had missed DuBois, since his goings and comings were nebulous at best.

"Yes, my chief. Red Horse discovered them this morning."

LeFever rose quickly.

"Come. Show me. Have you told anyone?"

"No."

"Good. Then let us look. Mandan, you say? I am not surprised!"

Outside, they encountered the black slave.

"Come with us," Blue Jacket spoke sharply, in French. "Bring two blankets!"

The bewildered Paint quickly stepped back inside, picked up a couple of blankets, and hurried after the others. It was not his place to ask questions.

A short while later, he understood. The four men managed, with great difficulty, to remove the

Mandan lance and disentangle the bodies, frozen in grotesque positions by the rigor of death. Flies were beginning to gather. They laid out the corpses as best they were able, and covered them with the blankets. They could be wrapped and tied for decent burial later.

Paint stood beside Red Horse, his face shiny with perspiration and his eyes still wide with horror and amazement.

"I told you, Horse . . . this woman was trouble!"

26
>> >> >>

There were two more funerals, two more graves on the grassy slope behind the fort. To the survivors it must have seemed that the entire colony was being destroyed, a few persons at a time.

The connection between the trader's widow and the voyageur, DuBois, was poorly understood, and for the sake of decency, LeFever intended to keep it that way. The official statement was that the two had been killed by a native from upriver, who had escaped and was long gone before the bodies were discovered. The assailant had been identified as a Mandan, by the weapon that he left behind.

That part was essential in order to prevent accusation directed toward any other natives. It would be possible, even, that some of the colony, or the voyageurs, could place blame on their friendly Kenza neighbors. With that possibility in mind, LeFever walked down to the voyageurs' camp for a brief council. He found that he had little to fear on that score. Although DuBois had been respected as a strong leader, he had apparently not been well liked as a man. The captain could detect no hint of desire for vengeance.

"He got what he earned," a glum adventurer observed, as he sat cross-legged by his cooking fire.

This seemed to be the general feeling. Some of the voyageurs were already packing up, preparing to start downriver. With their loss of leadership, the prospects for trade or profit here were rapidly diminishing.

There was rumor, of course, about the trader's wife. Many of the voyageurs must have had some understanding of her relationship with DuBois. They would, of course, talk with soldiers and civilians from the post, and the rumors would spread. It is doubtful, however, that even those with the greatest knowledge suspected the depth of the plot. None guessed that the murder of the trader was part of the illicit affair. Even LeFever, with his extra insight after viewing the bodies, never pieced that together. It continued to be regarded as a separate incident. Possibly Paint, with his keen insight into human nature, and his quiet powers of observation, might have suspected. If so, he never voiced his thoughts.

Now Captain LeFever was faced with a major decision. What should he report to the governor? He was faced with a completely unwanted decision. How could he decide what might well be the future or the demise of Fort de Chastaigne?

On the positive side, he had made many valuable contacts, and the establishment of a fur trade seemed favorable. DuBois, the man who had seemed the greatest threat to such trade, was dead. He had no doubt that DuBois' death would end any animosity among the Mandans.

He had managed to lay the groundwork for Santa Fe trade. He had made allies of tribes who had traded there already, and a guide who had been to Santa Fe was available. It was still possible to mount an expedition to Santa Fe this season.

On the negative side, however, there were many bleak points to ponder. Several apparently unrelated incidents had demoralized the little colony. One in ten of the settlers had died, in the most tragic and gruesome manner. The survivors were depressed, pessimistic, and already talking failure.

The trader was dead, and his employees, with no supervision, were floundering aimlessly. Of course, a new franchisee would be appointed, but it would take time.

The powder magazine was gone, with the loss of its contents. It would seem that they should not start for Santa Fe without a new supply. It would be foolhardy. For that matter, LeFever was increasingly wondering if he should try to leave at all, with morale at such a low ebb. The way things had been happening for the past few weeks, he had grave doubts.

Well, he must do something. Any decision was better than none, in a crisis. A commander in the military, he had observed, will often be more easily forgiven for a poor decision than for no decision at all. Yes, that might help morale, to appear to be moving forward.

He recalled White Fox to his office.

"We never finished our council, my friend," he greeted. "There were other matters."

"*Aiee*, yes!" agreed Fox. "Many things."

He had been greatly impressed by the explosion of the powder house. Although he was already outside the palisade, the roar was deafening, and the flash of light like a hundred spears of real-fire in a storm. White Fox had already been aware that this medicine was strong, but had never seen such a demonstration of its power. He hoped never to again. Like other things of the whites, this medicine could be good or bad, depending on its use. If used for good, such as hunting or defense . . . well, he had seen good things.

This accident was not a good thing. It caused him to recall an incident that had once been told to him. A holy man of another tribe, it was said, had used his medicine to bring evil to a rival. The rival was destroyed, dying a mysterious death, but in half a moon the perpetrator was also dead. White Fox had increasingly come to respect the responsibility that falls upon those with the gift.

The stronger a holy man's medicine, he now thought, the more dangerous its misuse. And he was still slightly puzzled that, with all the powerful medicines of the French, there seemed to be no keeper of the medicine.

The Spanish in Santa Fe had had holy men, he remembered, but they had seemed to be part of the problem. Again, was it misuse of their powerful gift that had caused the pueblo war? The whites seemed to have much trouble with this.

"Fox," Blue Jacket said, "we must decide quickly about Santa Fe."

"Yes, that is true."

"Now, many things must still be decided, but we can make some plans. Will you help buy horses?"

"From the Kenzas?"

"Yes . . . to trade, later, from your people, if it seems good."

"May Red Horse help? He is good with horses."

"Of course. As you wish. I will send the sergeant with you, so that the Kenzas know you buy for us."

"It is good. When do you wish this?"

"Soon. Today?"

White Fox nodded.

"It is good. We will begin."

This was a satisfying turn of things. The inactivity . . . no, the indecisiveness of the situation, had begun to be worrisome to the people from the prairie. All three of them had begun to long for the predictability of the big open sky and the grassland.

"How many horses?" he asked.

"Oh . . . I had not decided. We should take maybe a dozen soldiers, no?"

"Maybe so. Fifteen or twenty horses, then? Some for packs?"

"Yes, go ahead. It may be a few days before we can start."

Fox nodded. He realized that it would take a little while for messengers to return from the next chief up. A strange custom.

Red Horse was delighted at the prospect of some horse trading. What better way to spend a few days while waiting to see what would come next? White Fox, while not quite so vocal about it, was almost equally pleased. The sergeant joined them, and the three men walked the few hundred paces to the Kenza village. By inquiry, and with the help of Lame Beaver, they found a couple of men who might have horses to trade, and proceeded to where the animals were held.

By evening they had negotiated for several, marking each with a handprint of paint on the left shoulder.

"Can we leave them here until we finish trading?" asked Fox, as shadows grew long. South Wind would begin to expect their return.

"Yes," answered the Kenza. "You will come back in the morning?"

It was agreed, and they made their way back to the fort.

After another day's trading they had accumulated a total of eighteen horses, and the trading began to lag. The remaining horses seemed to fall into two classes. The animals that the Kenzas were willing to trade were of poor quality. And those of good quality were not for sale.

"It is enough," White Fox decided. "We will take these, and get more from our people."

Over all, he was pleased. Some of the animals were quite acceptable. He had chosen a blue roan gelding for himself, and a gentle-eyed dun mare for South Wind. Red Horse was still busily sorting his favorites from among the little herd. They drove them to a little meadow near the fort.

"You are to herd them," he told Red Horse. The responsibility would be good for the young man.

Somewhat to Fox's surprise, Red Horse received permission for Paint to assist with the herd. That, too, was good. Red Horse had seen an easier way, and had taken initiative to use it.

Maybe this summer would result in good things, after all. Horse had already learned much, of both good and bad.

27

»» »» »»

It all happened very quickly. Captain LeFever had expected a courier from the governor, but hardly this sort of attention.

The canoe, manned by adroit boatmen, slid to a stop below the fort. The man in the front jumped to shore, and pulled the prow up onto the bank. In the center of the craft sat a tall, uniformed officer, who now stood and made his way forward. LeFever could not be certain of the man's insignia at this distance, but watched closely as he started up the slope.

The officer carried himself well, a professional military man. A bit older than himself, LeFever thought. Possibly outranking him, at least in grade. A suspicious dread gnawed at his vitals. Why would the governor send an officer who ranked the commandant to visit a post, unless that commandant was in trouble? He had nervously considered this possibility, but saw no way that he could have prevented this whole bizarre series of events. No, surely that was not it. Yet the officer striding up toward the fort was unmistakably a man of authority. If not a staff officer, certainly accustomed to giving orders.

The newcomer approached the gate and the sentry saluted smartly. Good! At least that would present a good first impression. The officer tossed a casual salute in return, and continued his way across the compound. LeFever stepped from the headquarters building to meet him. A captain, he could now see . . . the same rank, but older . . . what . . . ?

The new captain paused only a moment to glance at the crater where the powder house once stood, hardly breaking stride as he moved on. He saw LeFever and stepped toward him, with a friendly smile, saluting as he did so.

"Captain LeFever? Captain Derome, here. *Sacrebleu*, that must have been a blast, no?"

"Yes, Captain, quite a blast."

What was this about? Why didn't the man get on with it? He didn't come all the way from the governor to make small talk about the accident.

Derome was taking a letter from his tunic, and LeFever recognized the governor's seal.

"Here are your orders, Captain," the newcomer said, extending the letter.

"Orders? You are replacing me?"

"Me? Oh, no, I am here to help you. We are to close the post."

"Then I *am* in trouble?"

"No, I think not . . . the governor seemed pleased with the way you have handled your emergency."

"But why, then . . . am I to be reprimanded?"

"No, no reprimand. But look at this from the governor's point, LeFever. So much has gone wrong here. Maybe just a bad-luck post . . . better to start over, no? Oh yes, they were pleased about DuBois. Not his real name, of course."

"What . . . who was he?"

"Can't remember at the moment. Fugitive from justice . . . Quebec, as I recall. Broke jail or something. They've been looking for him."

"But Captain, I did nothing to apprehend him."

"True," Derome answered with a chuckle, "but someone did, and in your command. Your jurisdiction, that is. Mandan, I heard? Saved the Crown a bit of nuisance, no?"

So, he was not to be demoted, or relieved of command. That, at least, was favorable. But, the unfinished exploration, the trade with the tribes upriver . . . Santa Fe! He would be transferred somewhere, and all he had begun would be wasted.

"Captain Derome," he began, hesitantly, "I have begun good work, here. I have talked to men who have been to Santa Fe! They can take me there."

"Yes," mused Derome. "Quite so. That must

have been in your report, was it not? Maybe that is why the governor wishes to see you."

"See me?"

"Yes. You are to report to him, while I help your staff close down here."

"But what . . . ?"

"I do not know, Captain. Maybe . . . Have you some brandy, LeFever? It has been a long day."

The orders contained very little information, except that he was to report to the governor after the arrival of "the Bearer," Captain Derome.

"I know that the prospect of international trade with Spain intrigues him," Derome said confidentially, after a drink or two. "That is my guess . . . he wants to ask you to head that up."

Well, so be it, thought LeFever. *I could do that.* Not this season, perhaps, but maybe next. Who knows?

Suddenly he was eager to talk to the governor, to tell of the exciting possibilities he had uncovered. Yes, he would look forward to starting back tomorrow. There were a few things he must do . . . talk to the Kenzas . . . to White Fox . . . yes, it would be good to nurture that contact . . .

A few days later, White Fox, South Wind, and Red Horse rode across the Sacred Hills toward the Ar-kenzas and the summer camp of the Southern band. Red Horse, after much deliberation, had chosen for himself a spotted gelding, white with rosettes of red, and also a copper-colored mare.

Blue Jacket had been very generous as he left. The people from the prairie did not fully understand, except that the messenger had come and Blue Jacket said that he must go to hold council with their chief. The French were to leave the fort. That seemed a matter of great importance to the French, somehow. It seemed of little consequence to the People, who left their settlement at least twice each year.

Blue Jacket seemed to think he would return, and was still interested in Santa Fe. For now, he was mostly interested in hurrying to the council with his chief. But he had been generous. Two horses for each of them, a fine knife for White Fox and another for Red Horse. He had offered such a knife to South Wind, but she smiled, shook her head, and showed him her flint knife, which she had had so long. Blue Jacket laughed, and gave her a highly polished metal mirror, as well as some beads, trinkets, and other trade goods.

Now they were in familiar country. Red Horse was looking ahead eagerly, trying to see the first sign of smoke from the cooking fires. They should reach the band's camp sometime today . . .

It was well past noon when the first bluish smudge on the distant prairie told that their goal was in sight. It would still be a long time before they reached the camp. Nearly dark, maybe.

"May I go on ahead?" asked Red Horse, impatient as usual.

White Fox smiled.

"Yes, go on. Be careful . . . easy on your horse!"

The young man put heels to his spotted gelding and raced away, not at a sprint, but at a gentle, ground-eating lope. White Fox knew that the boy was too much of a horseman to abuse the animal. In fact, he was slightly embarrassed at having mentioned it. Well, there was no harm. He smiled at South Wind, and they rode on, at a more leisurely pace.

Red Horse and Blue Swallow walked along the stream above the camp. His parents had not yet arrived, but surely would soon. He had wanted to reach the camp first because there was so much to tell. He had stopped at the lodge of Red Feather, to quickly tell him of the summer, and then set out immediately to look for Swallow. He found her easily.

"I heard you were back," she said shyly.

She was more beautiful than he remembered. Much more so than the Mandan Girl-Who-Smiled. How could he have thought they looked alike? And the blue-eyed wife of the trader . . . so exciting, intriguing.

He and Swallow walked along the stream, enjoying each other's companionship. It was not necessary to say much, beyond exchanging news.

He told her of the exciting events at the fort, and her dark eyes widened in wonder. She told him of their friends, White Hawk and Oak Leaf, who had married and were in their own lodge.

"*Aiee!*" he laughed. "Married! It is good!"

Then he became embarrassed and confused, because he had meant that *that* marriage was good, and Swallow might think that he meant . . . But Swallow pretended not to notice, and they fell silent, merely enjoying the moment.

"My parents should be here soon," Red Horse said. "Maybe I should go and see."

But, he made no move to do so.

"When you were at the Mandan towns," Swallow asked mischievously, "were there pretty women?"

Red Horse remembered the hurt he had felt when the Girl-Who-Smiled had been with another. Now, it was almost amusing.

"None like you," he said truthfully.

For some reason, the advice of Black Paint came back to him.

There are many kinds of women, Paint had said.

What else had he said? *A man must learn these things for himself, and when he has learned, he will understand.* Well, in this summer of learning, Red Horse had certainly seen some different women. He had been excited, intrigued, hurt, disappointed. None of it could compare with the fullness in his chest and the warmth he felt toward the young woman at his side now. He slipped his arm around the slender waist as they walked, and she leaned closer. This was his friend, first and foremost, a person he could trust.

"None like you," he repeated silently, with a great deal more meaning than even Paint might have understood.

GENEALOGY

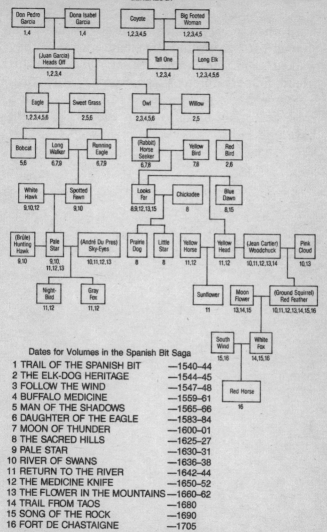

Dates for Volumes in the Spanish Bit Saga

1	TRAIL OF THE SPANISH BIT	—1540–44
2	THE ELK-DOG HERITAGE	—1544–45
3	FOLLOW THE WIND	—1547–48
4	BUFFALO MEDICINE	—1559–61
5	MAN OF THE SHADOWS	—1565–66
6	DAUGHTER OF THE EAGLE	—1583–84
7	MOON OF THUNDER	—1600–01
8	THE SACRED HILLS	—1625–27
9	PALE STAR	—1630–31
10	RIVER OF SWANS	—1636–38
11	RETURN TO THE RIVER	—1642–44
12	THE MEDICINE KNIFE	—1650–52
13	THE FLOWER IN THE MOUNTAINS	—1660–62
14	TRAIL FROM TAOS	—1680
15	SONG OF THE ROCK	—1690
16	FORT DE CHASTAIGNE	—1705

Dates are only approximate, since the People have no written calendar.
Characters in the Genealogy appear in the volumes indicated.

A proud people in a proud land

The Spanish Bit
Saga

Set in the New World of the sixteenth and seventeenth centuries, Don Coldsmith's acclaimed novels re-create a time, a place, and a people that have been nearly lost to history. In the SPANISH BIT SAGA we see history through the eyes of the proud Native Americans who lived it.

Turn the page for an exciting preview of WORLD OF SILENCE, a Spanish Bit Super Edition, to be published in February 1992. It will be available wherever Bantam Books are sold.

1

>> >> >>

As a child, Possum never doubted that he was loved. It is strange, perhaps, even to question the amount or intensity of such a nebulous thing as love. It is a thing that cannot be weighed or measured, only felt. It is a thing of the spirit, as real as the spirit of a budding tree, or new grass in the Moon of Greening. Or a sunset, a distant storm over the plain, or the laughter of clear water over white gravel shoals in a prairie river. All of these are things of the spirit, like . . . like love. Not only seen or heard or tasted or touched, but *felt*, in the fullness of spirit that is known to those who love and are loved.

Though one cannot measure the extent of love, it was apparent that there had never been a child among the People whose parents loved him more. This was an idyllic union, admired, sometimes envied by others of the Eastern band. Possum's mother, Otter Woman, had been a Warrior Sister, sworn to chastity until she chose to resign her high position to marry.

She could have continued for several more years if she chose. The honor of this office was great, and she performed it well. The dance steps, the ceremonies, the elaborate costuming, all seemed designed with this young woman in mind. Her tall form and graceful movements were greatly admired by all, both members of the warrior society and the spectators. There had never been a Warrior Sister so skilled, so well suited to the position. Or so beautiful, it was said.

Any one of many young warriors would have gladly died for her, both those in the Elk-dog Society and in the other warrior societies, the Bow-strings and the Bloods. It was no great surprise, however, when she chose Walking Horse, a young man of the Elk-dogs. He came from a prominent family, that of Red Feather, an important chief of the band back in the days of the Blue Paints War. Horse was surely destined for greatness, but remained as humble and friendly as if he did not even know about it.

These two young people had been friends since their childhood together in the Rabbit Society. They learned to swim, run, wrestle, to use weapons, and to ride with skill. When, at puberty, they graduated into the diverse worlds of men and women, these two remained good friends. Others of their age paired off and established their own lodges, but these two seemed in no hurry. Such a friendship needs no proof, but stands by itself.

This one had lasted so long, however, that the entire band was relieved when it came to fruition. Otter Woman resigned her position as Warrior Sister to marry Walking Horse, and the People rejoiced with them and for them. A union based solidly on a friendship that already exists is a good one, the old women told each other. And it seemed true. The love between these two handsome young people shone in their eyes and in their actions. The People laughed and made jokes, but they were pleased, and sometimes envious of this happy couple.

A child of such love will also be loved, and it was so with Possum, who was born the following season. It was not that he was such a beautiful child, for he was not. But he was born with the wide-eyed, knowing stare that some infants have, already old and wise, yet inquisitive about new surroundings. Beyond that, his face was narrow and long, and carried a droll expression of underlying amusement at the strangeness of all things. The first thing that anyone noticed about the child, however, was his hair. Many infants are bald, some have hair that lies close to the head like a fur cap. This hair, nearly three finger-breadths long, stood erect, bristling in all directions. In addition, it was not quite the jet-black color that was familiar to the People. An occasional infant was born with hair of a lighter shade from the influx of blood from outsiders. There had been intermittent contact with Spanish, French, and with other tribes through the generations. Usually the baby hair gave way to a color that was uniformly dark. At least, not noticeably different. It would undoubtedly occur in this case, and the color was no detriment. Many of the People, in fact, proudly traced their family back to Heads-Off, an outsider who brought the First Elk-dog to the Southern band, and became a subchief.

The child would probably be a handsome man, too. Both parents were quite attractive. But that was in the future. Just now his appearance was amusing. Nearly everyone who saw the infant was made to smile. The wide-eyed, solemn, yet amused expression, the bristling hair that stood erect like . . .

"His hair is like that of a porcupine," chuckled Walking Horse.

"No, no," said Otter Woman in mock rebuke. "It does not bristle with quills! It is soft fur, like that of a possum."

So, the child became Possum. It was a baby name, one that would be discarded soon anyway. But it was bestowed with love, which was apparent to all, and especially to Possum.

Such a child, loved by his parents and amusing to all, responds well to the actions of others. Possum smiled early. As others smiled, chuckled, or laughed, he began to do so in response. He regarded everyone as his friend, and related to all with delight. He grew chubby and happy, nourished not only by the breasts of his mother but by the extra nutrition of the spirit . . . the love of all who knew him. He returned that affection with a love of his own, a love for everyone he met. That in itself was ironic, in light of later events in his life.

It was in the Moon of Awakening that he became ill. That, too, was ironic. A small infant, one might suppose, would be most subject to illness in the dark moons of winter. Possum, of course, was sheltered and protected and well cared for, and prospered through that period, even the Moon of Hunger.

It had grown quite warm on several sunny days before the end of the Moon of Awakening. But Cold Maker, saving one last sally for the end, swept down once more, coating the prairie with ice and blowing his chilling breath. It was a chill that seemed to penetrate through and through, clear to the bone. The People hovered over their lodge-fires and waited for Sun Boy to return and drive Cold Maker back to the Northern Mountains and his caves of ice.

And it happened, of course. It has always been so. But the

People were weary of winter's cold, and their spirits were vulnerable. The changes, from cold to warm, then cold and warm yet again was too much for mere human flesh to bear. A sickness raced through the camp, striking down old and young alike. A sudden cough, a rapid warming of the skin, and increasing difficulty in breathing. There were those who insisted that two different spirits were involved. One attacked the elders, filling their lungs and choking their ability to move air in and out. The other was limited to the young. It was a particularly severe form of an illness that sometimes struck the children. It, too, was accompanied by a cough, fever, and difficulty in breathing. Some died from this, too, their skins reddened and blotchy, hot to the touch in their last days.

The holy men did not attempt to explain the differences, but only assisted as best they could. Dances, prayers, and chants of supplication. Plant powders in the lodge-fires to produce pungent smoke. Sweat-lodge ceremonies, which seemed to help some with the lung congestion. There were also potions and teas to help the cough and reduce fever.

Despite all these efforts, the Song of Mourning was heard almost constantly. The very old and the very young were hard hit, of course.

One old warrior, half blind and infirm, challenged the spirits that had claimed his grandson. He arrayed himself for battle, painted his face, and walked out into the chill of the night, singing. It was not the Mourning Song that floated back to the ears of the distant listeners, but the Death Song:

> The Grass and the Sun go on
> forever,
> But today is a good day to
> die.

It was a statement of intention, a declaration that he intended to die fighting this thing that was killing the People. Perhaps his death would appease whatever spirits were claiming the old and the young.

Finally he was heard no more. His body was found later, where he had fallen facedown, apparently in mid-stride, fighting for breath as his own lungs failed.

Who is to say what turned the course of the battle? The

chants and potions of the holy men, or the Death Song of old Red Snake? Maybe the combined prayers of all the families whose old and young had fallen ill. At any rate, the battle had turned. There were fewer new cases. With the warming days, those still ailing were brought out into the sunlight, and this, too, seemed to hasten their recovery.

But it was too late for Possum. One of the last to be struck down, the infant hovered between life and death. Otter Woman slept little, and then only fitfully and for short periods. Mostly she held the baby, rocking and crooning to him, and praying.

The holy man performed his rituals and prescribed a syrup of plant teas and honey, but he was not encouraging. He said very little, but it was apparent that he was exhausted. It must have been many days since he had been able to rest. Otter Woman felt sorry for him as he finished the ceremonies and shuffled away. But she feared that he had said little because he held little hope for the infant Possum.

The child lay near death for four days and nights, while his mother hovered, rocked, fanned, crooned, and bathed the fevered face. The blotchy roughness of hot dry skin persisted, and it was difficult not to despair. Possum no longer took the nipple well, and her breasts became engorged and tender. She knew that when he began to improve, he must have nourishment, so her breasts must continue to produce. To keep the flow coming, she milked it out with her fingers, catching the flow in a small gourd. She managed to feed a little to the sick infant from the gourd each time, sacrificing the rest to the fire. Maybe that would appease the hungry spirits that were devouring the children. Anyway, it could do no harm.

Of most concern to her was the look on the infant Possum's face. Where he had always worn a look of amused understanding, now his facial expression was one of worry. Of *terror*, almost. He no longer smiled. Day after day, his fever and labored breathing were accompanied by the pained, anxious expression. It was as if the child *knew* of his desperate battle for life, and was uncertain whether anyone could help him. Otter Woman sometimes had the strange feeling that *he* knew what to do but was unable to communicate it to her.

"Tell me, my child," she whispered when they were alone. *"What must I do?"*

The infant would stare into her face with burning dark eyes

and whimper softly, nothing more. Then she would fall into an exhausted sleep, and wake again with no answers.

At last came a morning when she awoke, frantic that she had slept too long. There was no sound from the child. His eyes were closed. *He is dead!* she thought, reaching to touch the tiny face. But it was not cold. Cool, yes. The fever had broken. The big dark eyes opened now, and the infant looked straight into her face. There was a new look. The frantic, terror-filled stare that was so frightening had changed. The old look, of amusement and understanding, flickered there. Weakly, but it was there.

Then, that most beautiful of all sights . . . the infant smiled. He had not done so for days. Weeping, she gathered him into her arms and cradled him, rocking gently. Eagerly, he turned toward her and she opened the front of her mothering-shirt to put him to breast. He sucked hungrily, draining the life-giving fluid. Her body responded, and she smiled when the other breast began to leak in unison.

"Your time will come," she whispered softly as she wiped the spill from her shirt. "Our man-child eats again now!"

Walking Horse entered the lodge, and she called to him excitedly.

"Look! The fever is gone . . . he feeds!"

Horse dropped to his knees beside her, and the two clung to each other, their tears of joy mingling while the tiny Possum continued to feed noisily.

"We must give thanks," she murmured.

"Yes. At the Sun Dance . . . we will make a good sacrifice."

"What?"

"I do not know. We must consider. A horse, maybe?"

Otter Woman smiled. "I do not know. We will speak of it later. For now, our joy is enough."

And it was good.

2

>> >> >>

The Sun Dance was especially meaningful that year. The family of the Real-chief had procured a magnificent bull for the ceremonial effigy. Its fur was dark and thick, especially fine for this late in the season. The head had been propped facing the east, and the effigy of logs and brush, with the skin stretched over it, was so lifelike that there was much comment.

That was good, for this must be a special Sun Dance. Everyone had been affected by the illness that had swept through the winter camps of the People, three moons before. The Eastern band had been hardest hit, with nearly every family either in mourning or rejoicing that they had been spared. There were many bittersweet reunions with relatives from other bands, people clinging together and weeping in the sharing of their grief.

Those whose loved ones had been spared, like Otter Woman and Walking Horse, offered gifts and prayers of thanksgiving. Three fine furs they had chosen to sacrifice in appreciation for the survival of their son. An otter, dark and shiny, a thick soft beaver, and a beautifully colored foxskin were offered. Ceremonially, the couple walked to the west end of the brush-roofed medicine lodge where the buffalo effigy stood. Slowly, with great emotion, Walking Horse tied each skin in turn to the poles of the open-sided lodge. As Otter Woman handed each symbol of their gratitude to her husband, there was a hushed murmur among the onlookers. The People were impressed by the value and the beauty of the gifts. These sacrifices were of the best, befitting the status of this couple, as well as the depth of their gratitude.

Many other sacrifices were made that season. There were beautifully carved and decorated prayer sticks, garments, footwear, a blanket. One warrior gave up his favorite bow to fulfill a vow. He had promised this to atone for the survival of his beloved young wife. Another promised a horse, to be left behind at the end of the last day of ceremonies. Surely the prayers that accompanied such lavish sacrifices reached appropriate deities. It was a time of thanksgiving.

There were, of course, prayers of entreaty also, and vows of penitence if only this would be a better year than the one just past. And above all, there was the basic theme of the Sun Dance: joyous celebration for the return of the Sun, the grass, and in turn, the buffalo.

This was Possum's first Sun Dance, of course. Not yet a full year old, much of his understanding had yet to come. Still, the toddler was impressed by the whole scene. He had never seen so many people before. And, since this was a child who had always loved people and the communication with other human beings, the youngster was in his glory. He wore a broad smile during the entire five days of the celebration.

Of course, he received much attention, as a pleasant child does. His friendly smile, his droll expressions, all attracted more attention. In addition, the story of his having been spared from near death by the fever was well known. Friends and relatives from other bands came to offer congratulations and after-fact sympathy for the dreadful experience. Each of these spent time laughing and playing with the child. Many times, Otter Woman answered the same question.

"Why is he called Possum?"

Patiently, she explained. The reason was not so evident now. His hair had grown darker and longer. It was long enough, in fact, that it was possible to begin to plait the locks after the manner of the People. Slender strips of otterskin were braided into the plait, to lengthen and fill out the total effect. The otter strips would be worn until his own hair was long enough to complete the effect. This made Possum look even more like a wise old man. It also, however, completely destroyed the reason for his baby name. For a while, Otter Woman explained it to each questioner. Finally, she decided it was useless. One who had not seen the infant's appearance simply could not understand.

"It is only a name," she would reply now, and that seemed to suffice. For her, he would always be Possum, her baby, anyway. Besides, at his First Dance at the age of two years, he would receive a new name.

Meanwhile, she would continue to rejoice in the fact that he was *alive.* What a blessing, to have come so close to losing him. *Aiee!* She shuddered at the thought, and held him close again, as if she would never let go.

He was beginning to walk some now, which was worrisome. All the confusion and excitement of the Sun Dance, the hundreds of people milling around day and night, the horses and dogs. . . . Otter Woman was anxious lest the toddler wander off and be stepped on in the excitement. She need not have worried . . . all of the People looked after all children, their own and others'. She knew this, but this child was *hers.* People smiled at her maternal protectiveness, and understood. She had nearly lost this child.

Walking Horse was pleased at the child's reactions to the entire Sun Dance celebration. Possum seemed interested in watching, and not in the least alarmed by all the noise and confusion. There was always a great deal of yelling and shouting, especially around the area where impromptu horse races were always taking place. Many infants were frightened by this noisy pastime, but not Possum. He watched the proceedings with the same delight that was evident in everything he observed.

At last, the Sun Dance was over, and the bands went their separate ways. It was necessary to do so. The People had prospered in recent generations, and had grown. It had been a time of relative peace, since they had become allies with the Head Splitters, their former enemies. That was long ago, now. The two nations had joined against a greater foe, the Blue Paints from the north.

With no enemies, both nations had prospered. With no casualties in battle, population had increased, and larger seasonal hunts were possible. The Head Splitters were frequent visitors, often taking part in the Sun Dance of the People, since they had none of their own. But the increase in numbers at the Sun Dance led to other problems. The grass needed for the hundreds of horses that gathered each season became scarce very quickly. Likewise, there was a limit to availability of food and water. Hundreds of people require a great quantity of food, and game soon became scarce.

Once, it was said, the gathering for the Sun Dance lasted nearly a full moon. Now, it was necessary to split up and move apart to avoid a shortage of food and grass for the horses. The first of the big lodges came down the day after the final ceremonies were completed. The Mountain band was the first to go. Theirs was the longest journey. By evening, however, the Red Rocks had headed west in their long, ragged column, their baggage piled on pole-drags. The visiting Head Splitters accompanied them, since their territories more closely approximated each other.

The Southern band was in no hurry to go, since the gathering was in their own range this season. They began to pack in a leisurely fashion.

The Eastern band, too, had a shorter distance to travel, but they began preparations. They had been, for many generations, the butt of ethnic jokes. Those of the Eastern band were regarded as foolish people, bad luck people. No one knew how it had started . . . possibly because of their slightly different terrain and proximity to the woodlands. Anyone who found himself in a ridiculous situation was sure to be teased, even in the other bands. A man who had been bested in a horse trade, for instance, might overhear a conversation: "Well, you know, his grandfather was of the Eastern band."

There were ribald jokes and stories about the Eastern band. The first horses they obtained, for instance, they led around for a long time before they learned that they were to be ridden. In the other bands even now, a common remark concerning a lame, blind, or otherwise useless horse might be: "Maybe you can sell it to the Eastern band."

There had been a concerted effort on the part of Red Feather, their great leader, to live down this reputation for foolishness. He had met with some degree of success, and gained respect, but it was not complete. The band still worked hard to avoid the jibes that were so quick to come. It was good not to be the last to arrive for the Sun Dance: ("They just found their way here.") Or the last to leave: (Are they *still* not organized?")

So, by common understanding and generations of slighting

remarks, it had become custom. The Eastern band would strike their lodges not first or last, but somewhere between. They were ready to depart shortly after Sun Boy reached the top of his run.

"Where do we camp tonight?" asked Otter Woman. She lifted young Possum to the back of one of the dependable old pack mares and tied him in place.

"Medicine River," Horse answered. "So they say, anyway. It is good. There should be water and grass."

"Not at the Rock?"

"No, no."

"Good. That place bothers me."

Walking Horse laughed.

"It bothers many people. That is why people avoid it."

Medicine Rock had a big part in the tradition of the People. It was there, it was said, that Eagle, the great storyteller of long ago, had spent a winter with Old Man himself, while his broken leg had healed. Many did not believe it. The place had always had a reputation for supernatural happenings, however, even before that. There was no doubt that its spirit was strange. It had been of benefit to some, accounting for Eagle's survival in the old legend.

Then again Medicine Rock had been the site of the final defeat of the invading Blue Paints. By the combined strength of the medicines of two young holy men, one of the People and the other from the Head Splitters . . . It was unclear how it had happened, but those two caused a mighty herd of buffalo to push the enemies over the cliff to their deaths.

Since that time the People avoided the area. The brooding appearance of the gray stone, already noted for strange spirits, added to the knowledge that many enemy spirits had departed from human bodies in that place. There were some who professed to be unafraid. But when the time came to exhibit courage, even they were hesitant. Why take chances? one asked offhandedly. There were better places to camp or to hunt.

The traveling band passed the cliff on the other side of the river, perhaps hurrying the horses a little to be far away by the time darkness fell. Three young men, goaded by the bravado of their inexperience, left the column to ride nearer the river and observe the face of the Medicine Rock cliff more closely.

They soon returned. No special reason, they insisted. A cliff is simply not very interesting. They raced forward to join the head of the column. Older and wiser people smiled at the folly of youth. They knew quite well that without the forbidding spirit of that rocky wall, those three youths would have spent all day exploring it.

They camped that night some distance to the east of the Medicine Rock. It was a beautiful camping place, downstream far enough to be free of the oppressive thoughts that clung to this stretch of Medicine River. Maybe it only seemed that the People stayed closer to the camp fires that evening, huddling near the warmth that was not really needed on this warm summer night.

Next morning they moved on toward the River of Swans, where they would camp for the summer. Otter Woman was glad to be moving away from the place. She felt somehow that its mysteries were linked to the future of her child, swaying happily on the back of the roan mare.

About the Author
>> >> >>

DON COLDSMITH was born in Iola, Kansas, in 1926. He served as a World War II combat medic in the South Pacific and returned to his native state where he graduated from Baker University in 1949 and received his M.D. from the University of Kansas in 1958. He worked at several jobs before entering medical school: he was a YMCA group counselor, a gunsmith, a taxidermist, and for a short time, a Congregational preacher. In addition to his private medical practice, Dr. Coldsmith is a staff physician at Emporia State University's Health Center, teaches in the English Department, and is active as a freelance writer, lecturer, and rancher. He and his wife of twenty-six years, Edna, have raised five daughters.

Dr. Coldsmith produced the first ten novels in "The Spanish Bit Saga" in a five-year period; he writes and revises the stories first in his head, then in longhand. From this manuscript he reads aloud to his wife, whom he calls his "chief editor." Finally the finished version is skillfully typed by his longtime office receptionist.

Of his decision to create, or re-create, the world of the Plains Indian in the sixteenth and seventeenth centuries, the author says: "There has been very little written about this time period.

I wanted also to portray these Native Americans as human beings, rather than as stereotyped 'Indians.' That word does not appear anywhere in the series—for a reason. As I have researched the time and place of the indigenous cultures, it's been a truly inspiring experience for me.''

A Proud People in a Harsh Land

THE SPANISH BIT
SAGA

Set on the Great Plains of America in the early 16th century, Don Coldsmith's acclaimed series recreates a time, a place and a people that have been nearly lost to history. With the advent of the Spaniards, the horse culture came to the people of the Plains. Here is history in the making through the eyes of the proud Native Americans who lived it.

☐ 26397-8	TRAIL OF THE SPANISH BIT	$3.50
☐ 26412-5	THE ELK-DOG HERITAGE	$3.50
☐ 26806-6	FOLLOW THE WIND	$3.50
☐ 26938-0	BUFFALO MEDICINE	$3.50
☐ 27067-2	MAN OF THE SHADOWS	$3.50
☐ 27209-8	DAUGHTER OF THE EAGLE	$3.50
☐ 27344-2	MOON OF THUNDER	$3.50
☐ 27460-0	SACRED HILLS	$3.50
☐ 27604-2	PALE STAR	$3.50
☐ 27708-1	RIVER OF SWANS	$3.50
☐ 28163-1	RETURN TO THE RIVER	$3.50
☐ 28318-9	THE MEDICINE KNIFE	$3.50
☐ 28538-6	THE FLOWER IN THE MOUNTAINS	$3.50
☐ 28760-5	TRAIL FROM TAOS	$3.50
☐ 29123-8	SONG OF THE ROCK	$3.50
☐ 29419-9	FORT DE CHASTAIGNE	$3.99
☐ 28334-0	THE CHANGING WIND	$3.95
☐ 28868-7	THE TRAVELER	$4.50

■■■■■■■■■■■■■■■■■■■■■■■■■■■■■■■

Available at your local bookstore or use this page to order.

TERRY C. JOHNSTON

Winner of the prestigious Western Writer's award, Terry C. Johnston brings you his award-winning saga of mountain men Josiah Paddock and Titus Bass who strive together to meet the challenges of the western wilderness in the 1830's.

☐ 25572-X **CARRY THE WIND–Vol. I** $5.50

☐ 26224-6 **BORDERLORDS–Vol. II** $5.50

☐ 28139-9 **ONE-EYED DREAM–Vol. III** $4.95

The final volume in the trilogy begun with *Carry the Wind* and *Borderlords*, ONE-EYED DREAM is a rich, textured tale of an 1830's trapper and his protegé, told at the height of the American fur trade.

Following a harrowing pursuit by vengeful Arapaho warriors, mountain man Titus "Scratch" Bass and his apprentice Josiah Paddock must travel south to old Taos. But their journey is cut short when they learn they must return to St. Louis...and old enemies.

Look for these books wherever Bantam books are sold, or use this handy coupon for ordering: